Believe in Me

Regena Bryant

Genesis Press, Inc.

INDIGO

An imprint of Genesis Press, Inc.
Publishing Company

Genesis Press, Inc.
P.O. Box 101
Columbus, MS 39703

All rights reserved. Except for use in any review, the reproduction or utilization of this work in whole or in part in any form by any electronic, mechanical, or other means, not known or hereafter invented, including xerography, photocopying, and recording, or in any information storage or retrieval system, is forbidden without written permission of the publisher, Genesis Press, Inc. For information write Genesis Press, Inc., P.O. Box 101, Columbus, MS 39703.

All characters in this book have no existence outside the imagination of the author and have no relation whatsoever to anyone bearing the same name or names. They are not even distantly inspired by any individual known or unknown to the author and all incidents are pure invention.

Copyright © 2012 Regena Bryant

ISBN-13: 978-1-58571-465-0
ISBN-10: 1-58571-465-8
Manufactured in the United States of America

First Edition

Visit us at www.genesis-press.com
or call at 1-888-Indigo-1-4-0

Dedication

To Paul for always believing in me.

Acknowledgements

Many thanks to the staff at Genesis Press for everything you do. To Sidney Rickman for another amazing editorial job. I appreciate all that you've taught me.

A million thanks to my friend and typo slayer Sonali Dev and an excellent beta reader Terry V.

My never ending thanks to the wonderful supportive fellowship of writers in the Windy City Chapter of RWA. I'm grateful for every one of you.

And my unending gratitude to Freedom Fighters everywhere for believing in shift.

Laus Deo!

Regena Bryant

Chapter 1

This was the last place she wanted to be. Alone on Thanksgiving eve, crying into a wine glass. How pathetic. Kitty Franklin glanced around the bar at the well-dressed crowd of Capitol Hill insiders and wannabes. She recognized many of the congressional office staffers gathered around the bar, and several had already approached her, status seekers and career political operatives hoping she might introduce them to her father, nineteen-term South Carolina Congressman Roosevelt Franklin. B. Smith's Union Station restaurant was a popular gathering place for the non-elected, working-class politicos of Washington, DC.

She raised her glass to the bartender, a silent request for one more.

"Can I buy you a drink?"

Kitty glanced over at the man sitting on the stool to her right. "No." She patted the American Express Platinum card that lay on the bar next to her left hand.

A wide grin covered the man's face. "Since it's like that, then you can buy me one. I'm Lemont Barnes."

"No," she said as she looked down her nose at his cheap suit.

"I see you're a woman of few words." Lemont gave a hollow chuckle.

"That's rich," Kitty said, more to her glass than him. She was sitting here because the opposite was true. She should have kept her mouth shut when her sisters inquired about their father's current affairs.

Yesterday her father had fired the executive director of the Franklin Family Life Center. He should have known better than to sleep with a member of his staff. Was he the only one who'd forgotten he'd almost lost an election ten years ago for a similar indiscretion?

"You're Congressman Franklin's daughter, right? I work on the Hill, in the old office building."

"That's nice," she murmured. Maybe she could practice holding her tongue with Lemont. Laughter from standing couples and groups awaiting tables for the restaurant's popular dinner service filled the room. The light jazz that had kept her company throughout the afternoon was barely audible now. She turned her back and let Lemont's weak rap bounce off her ears.

"Stuck-up bitch." He rose and moved through the crowd.

Now at least she had an example to prove her father wrong. She'd barely said a word, yet managed to piss Lemont off. Her father often praised her for speaking her mind, yet encouraged her to harness her tongue. He was the ultimate hypocrite. When he was her age he'd been an outspoken firebrand of a civil rights activist. Now, as a congressman, his life was full of silent innuendo and spoken half-truths.

She stared at the mirrored wall behind the bar and the profusion of multi-colored liquor bottles that lined the glass shelves. She caught her reflection between a bottle of bourbon and Chambord. Heat from the alcohol she'd consumed since three o'clock flushed her complexion. She cringed. Her skin was a color her mother might call ruddy. Her shoulder-length bob clung to her head like a military helmet. If she left now, she could go to one of DC's all-night hairdressers. Her mother, at least, would appreciate it if she looked presentable for tomorrow's family dinner. The rest of the family would most likely prefer her asking a hair weaver to sew her mouth shut.

Kitty hung her head and exhaled. "I'm not going to the family dinner tomorrow." She cast another glance around the room. There were a few singles scattered about the bar and the restaurant's waiting areas. Maybe she wasn't the only person who'd managed to piss off their entire family on the day before the holiday. No, they were probably just transplants from places too far away for them to make it home for the holidays. Some of them worked on a BlackBerry while others looked up every so often in hopeful anticipation as they waited for friends or loved ones.

If she weren't her father's personal attorney and secret keeper, she wouldn't be at odds with her sisters and alone tonight. She'd be enjoying the warmth of her mother's kitchen, maybe even helping with the preparations for tomorrow.

Instead of leaving when the barkeepers changed shifts at seven, she settled her bill and opened a new tab, with a new drink. "Amaretto stone sour, no fruit. And how about some chicken wings?"

"I think that's a good idea. I'll also bring you some bread and a glass of water." The second-shift bartender turned to place the order in the computer. He came back within minutes with the promised glass of water. "Miss Franklin, it's getting crowded in here, and not with a lot of our regulars. Why don't you put that card away? I'm not worried about you running out on your bill. Besides, I know your daddy."

"Thanks, Bobby." She raised her glass. "To Daddy, the cat with nine political lives." Helping her father slip past this latest scandal was going to take some cat-like legal agility.

She set the glass on the bar with a thud. Her father had paid Linda McNair handsomely to go away quietly. The plan was to have her replacement at the Franklin Family Life Center hired and a cover story in place for the media before the holiday weekend was over. But this morning she'd received notice that Linda McNair had filed suit. In addition to breach of contract, Linda claimed sexual harassment. When would her father learn that hell had no fury like a woman scorned? And when were these stupid women going to realize that the congressman would never leave his wife?

Kitty stared into the bar mirrors, at the fire in her eyes. The price she paid for making believe she was her father's son was too high.

"Those smell good." A strong male voice lifted her from her reverie.

She blinked. She hadn't noticed the arrival of her favorite appetizer. Thinking about her father's issues had consumed all of her attention.

"Have some." She pushed the plate of honey-glazed wings toward the occupant of the bar stool to her right.

"No, thank you, ma'am. I don't want to spoil my supper."

She swiveled on the bar stool to get a good look at her new neighbor, but couldn't quite make out all of his features. She tried to blame the bar's dim lighting, but knew it was the liquor. Though her focus was hazy, she detected a Southern kindness in the man's face. He flashed her a genuine smile from beneath a well-groomed mustache. She didn't think she recognized him, but his voice had a distinctly Southern drawl.

"Did my daddy send you?" Kitty's hand shook as she reached down to pick up a chicken wing.

"No, ma'am. I'm not from around here," he drawled.

She aimed the wing toward her mouth. "Ouch." The wing fell to the bar top. Her finger throbbed from her bite.

The polite stranger offered her a cocktail napkin.

"Shank you. You'd shink I'd know how to feed myself by now."
"Maybe you've had enough."
Her eyes narrowed. "Are you sure Daddy didn't send shu?"
"No, but maybe you should call your daddy and ask him to come pick you up."
Even impaired, her hearing detected something familiar in his voice. His vocal tone was similar to her father's. She turned away from the stranger and then looked back at him. "Maybe you should mind your own bishness," she snapped.
"Excuse me." The man swiveled on the bar stool. He picked up the change from his beer, stood, and strolled away.
Kitty turned back to mirror-gazing. She caught a glimpse of Bobby's watchful eye as he ran dirty glasses through the washing system. She'd had enough. As soon as she was stable enough to walk out of there with an ounce of decorum, she would.
But why hadn't her father sent someone to pick her up? He knew where she was. She sank closer to the bar. Tears burned her eyes. He was probably angry with her, too, because she'd told her sisters the truth. He liked to pretend they were a happy family, especially during the holidays.

Davis Thornton milled around the bar at B. Smith's with his beer, looking for space to stand. The restaurant buzzer in his left hand still displayed only one red dot. He put it back in his pocket. He was traveling alone so he could have eaten at the bar, but he'd been told it was worth the wait for a table in the main dining room. He looked again at the petite woman he'd sat next to at the bar. Nice looking lady, obviously trying to drown some pain. Hopefully, a friend or relative would come and see her home. He finished his beer and made his way through the crowd to the men's room.
"Man, what did you say to get Kitty Franklin to talk to you?"
Davis turned his head toward the man on his left, who was actually speaking to him while he completed his task at the urinal. "Who?"
"Didn't you know you were talking to Congressman Franklin's daughter? You must not work on the Hill," the man continued.
Davis zipped up his trousers. "Damn." That's why she looked so familiar.

"Yo, bro, if I were you I'd get back over there." A second man addressed him as he crossed over to the sinks. "Three young guns are about to pick her up. She must be drunk 'cause she hasn't run them off. And they don't look like they care who she is, if you get my drift."

How the hell had this happened? He did know her father. Dinner at B. Smith's had been Congressman Franklin's suggestion. Davis washed his hands and reached for a paper towel.

"Take some of those, my brother." A third man pointed to a jar of rainbow colored condoms on a shelf above the sink.

Davis caught his own bemused expression in the mirror. "Do you know her, too?"

"Know who?"

"The congressman's daughter."

"No, man, I'm a health educator. I'm just saying you don't tap nothing these days without a top hat."

Respectful of a man just doing his part, Davis reached in the jar and grabbed a handful of condoms.

"It don't take that much for that little bit," the health educator joked as he left the washroom.

Davis stood a few feet away from the bar and watched the three young men who surrounded Catherine Franklin. She was small and almost hidden by the broad-backed trio. They didn't look like thugs. Dressed in baggy-butt jeans, two of them sported jackets emblazoned with the Howard University mascot.

This really wasn't any of his business, but helping her could prove useful. Damn, one day in Washington and he was already corrupt, considering how he could turn doing the right thing into a political advantage. But it wouldn't be right to leave without helping her. Which way should he play this, fiancé or family? He hadn't noticed a ring on her finger earlier, and he did know her father. Davis noticed that the bartender had an eagle eye trained on her. He sprang into action.

"Excuse me, fellas."

The young men turned to face him, chests puffed out.

"What up, frat." Davis gave a second greeting to the one in the party who wore the classic black and gold colors of his fraternity. Up close, the fraternity crest on the front of the young man's rugby shirt encouraged him. The family ruse should work.

"What you want, man?" The roughest looking of the young men stepped to Davis. They stood toe to toe. Two men, six feet, three inches, sizing each other up in the middle of the bar. He looked the younger man in the eye, unfazed. What the youth lacked was experience and the backup that Davis had found behind the bar. Davis lifted his chin and nodded his head in response to the burly bartender's I got your back signal.

"It's time for me to take my sister home." The pager vibrated in his pocket. Davis turned toward her. "Let's go get something to eat. Mama won't appreciate you coming home in this condition."

"Won't say anything, never does." She bobbled on the barstool.

Thank God she's playing along. The roughest of the three stepped toward her and put his hand on her shoulder. "You can stay with us. We'll get you home."

She jerked back.

Davis cast a hard glance at all three young men. Two backed off. The bartender leaned over the bar and whispered something in the tough guy's ear. The young man backed away and the bartender motioned for Davis.

Once he satisfied the bartender's questions, Davis reached out and placed a light hand on her arm. "Let's go get something to eat, Catherine."

Chapter 2

After they were seated in the restaurant's elaborate dining room, Davis examined his surroundings. The place was magnificent. Elegant French doors stood as sentries for a glass-enclosed gallery. Period chandeliers hung from soaring, vaulted ceilings, and classic art deco pieces adorned the walls.

Kitty leaned forward, her head bobbling slightly. "How do you suddenly snow my name and why are you lookin' around like you've never been here before?"

Davis took a moment to consider her very direct questions. How should he answer? From her reaction in the bar, she was angry about something. And she was drunk. "This is my first time here."

"You know, this was once the presidential waiting rom, rom, room. Ish a national landmark."

"It's grand," he murmured. "Ms. Franklin…Catherine, there are some things I should tell you." He stopped to acknowledge the waiter who stood by their table.

"Are you ready to order?"

"The lady will have coffee, and I'd like a glass of ice water," Davis said.

"And some fried green tomatoes. They're a howse spec-specialty, since you're a first-timer." She leaned over the table and pointed a quivering finger in his direction. "I like how you take charge, a man of action. Now answer my question."

Davis thanked the waiter, then leaned back in his chair and took a deep breath. "My name is Davis Thornton…."

"I'm going to call you Ack-shun, Ack-shum Jackshun. Where you from?"

"Rock Hill, South Carolina, ma'am."

She leaned in closer, her breasts resting on the table. "I knew it. Daddy sent you. Are you a Secret Service agent?" she whispered conspiratorially.

Davis leaned in and matched her volume. "No, I'm not a Secret Service agent. Your father didn't send me, but I do know him."

She looked intently into his eyes for a moment, and then straightened in her chair. "Don't want to hear anything about it."

Her response puzzled him, and he took a moment to consider if he should press the issue. He didn't want her to become loud or belligerent. "I think you should know…"

She waved her hands for him to stop. "I know enough. I'll be back. Don't eat all the 'matoes." She stood up, steadied herself on the edge of the table, extended her left arm and hand like a tiller and a rudder and glided away.

In her wake Davis rubbed his chin and grinned at her ladylike struggle to pull it together. The lighting in the dining room was a bit brighter than the bar's, which gave him a clearer look at her features. Her skin was a very light brown, almost exactly the color of the buttery almond cookies he liked to purchase in Chicago's Chinatown. Her eyes, though cloudy from the alcohol, were a light topaz. She had a petite frame but when she leaned over the table she had looked a little top heavy. He lifted his eyes towards the ceiling and silently thanked God the lady looked nothing like her father.

"Your appetizer, sir."

The country boy in Davis caused him to part his lips in wonder as the waiter placed a platter of culinary artistry in the center of the table. The dish before him didn't look or smell anything like the fried green tomatoes his mother made. Golden-fried orbs, surrounded by a fragrant red sauce and arranged on a fancy plate, invited him to taste. He placed one morsel in his mouth and closed his eyes to savor the treat. This was Southern cooking with a twist. He turned to look behind him before enjoying another. He hoped he could heed her warning and not gobble up the tasty plate. An appreciative smile broke out across his face as his dinner companion approached the table. She looked even prettier now that she'd freshened her hair and makeup. He rose to assist with her chair. As he walked back to his side of the table, he completed his assessment. This was a Southern woman with a little twist.

She sat and drank two cups of coffee without saying a word. This gave him more time to consider how he might explain the coincidence of their meeting. When the waiter arrived to take their dinner orders, she responded without looking at the menu. "I'll have the shrimp and grits."

"Sounds interesting, I'll have the same."

Somewhere between the fried green tomatoes and the shrimp and grits, Kitty's focus cleared a bit. Thanks to the man of action sitting across from her, she was now a wide-awake drunk. But her brain wasn't functioning in its usual manner. She wasn't interested in what he did for a living or where he went to school. She didn't care if he belonged to a certain church or social organizations. She scanned his large hands. No ring.

"You're awful cut. Are you sure that's not a Secret Service body?"

Davis blushed and squirmed in his chair. "No, ma'am. There are some long, hard winters in Chicago and I had to do something to maintain. Working out is good for the mind, body, and soul."

"What was on your mind that worked you into that body?" She twirled her fork around on her plate. "Some fast Chi-town woman?"

"No, ma'am, those women didn't like a country boy's ways." He looked down. "It was my work that was on my mind. I work for a social services foundation. There's a lot of suffering in communities in the inner city, and working out helped me deal with it. But I'm sure you know all about it. Single parents, teenaged mothers, poverty, inadequate housing, imprisoned men, and crime."

"Some of us don't want help and some of us need to be locked up." She took another bite and wagged her fork at him. "I don't want to talk about that. Let's talk more about that body."

Davis shook his head. "I'd rather tell you more about my work."

"No, there's too much fine sitting in front of me to talk about work. I checked you out earlier when you walked away from me in the bar. I like your big Secret Service booty."

Davis swallowed hard. "Care for dessert?"

She leaned forward again. "No, I think you'll be sweet enough."

He coughed and tension spread across the table.

Kitty glanced at the dainty gold watch on her wrist. "Come on, Action, let's take a walk."

After a mad dash through Union Station's grand hall, Davis stood next to Kitty on the DC Metro red line train. They were surrounded by less than

Washington's elite. A homeless man sprawled across the seat behind them. The intensity of the man's musty odor burned his nose. "Is this safe?"

"You're here to protect me," she teased. "And this is our stop."

They stepped off the train and crossed a platform, went up one escalator, down another to catch another train. Davis's eyes darted around the people from all walks of life that hurried through the concrete bunkers of DC's Metro, even at this hour. He pulled his coat together as a subterranean chill raced up his back. The orange line train swooshed to a stop. Kitty reached for his hand and they hopped aboard.

Kitty plopped down on a compact plastic molded chair. He stood above her and analyzed the seat dimensions.

"Sit down, silly."

A wave of relief swept through him when he settled in beside her. A few years ago he would have needed both this seat and hers. He was still adjusting mentally and physically to his new looks. It was more common now for him to get appreciative looks and compliments from women, but Catherine Franklin's blatant admiration caught him a little off guard. She was really forward and she was working wonders for his self-esteem. He liked it. He liked her. The fat boy still hidden deep inside of him spoke up. You know she's too cute for us.

After a quick five-minute ride they exited at the Smithsonian stop. The air was crisp and cold as they walked down Fourteenth Street toward the National Mall. The little lady had to take two steps to his one to keep up with his long-legged stride. Since he didn't know where they were going, he slowed to a stroll and let her lead.

The warm, satisfying meal, combined with the coolness of the night, further cleared Kitty's senses. "Now if you like, you can tell me all about yourself. Is it really that cold in Chicago?"

"Yes, ma'am. That Hawk ain't nothing to play with. I didn't think I'd survive my first winter there."

She threaded her arm through his and snuggled up to him. "And what about the women? Why were they so cold to you, Action?" She looked up into his face and scooted in a little closer.

He'd been seriously overweight when he moved to Chicago five years earlier. But she wouldn't want to hear that.

"Are you always this forward?" he asked.

"I'm known to be direct."

Arm in arm, they crossed the street onto the grassy mall. Kitty pointed out their destination, the Washington Monument. As they strolled toward the obelisk, Davis spoke about his work at the Gates Foundation for Social Concerns.

"We try to help our people with life skills, education, and health care, whatever they need to help get on their feet and lead a fulfilling life."

"Do you provide any truth with that assistance?"

"What truth?" he asked.

"The truth that many of our problems, we bring on ourselves," she blurted out.

"I don't totally agree with you on that, but yes, it's a Baptist Methodist Assembly Church foundation. Self-help is central to our philosophy, very similar to your father's."

"You think?" She dropped his arm. "Do you know what dear Daddy was doing today?" She turned her head and muttered under her breath, "Besides throwing me under the bus."

"Yes, and now might be a good time for me to tell you."

She turned her face back towards him. "Oh, were you with him and his CBC buddies when they went across the bridge to give away turkeys and hams to the people?"

"No, ma'am, but that sounds like a good community service project."

"Nice photo op. Everybody having a happy holiday, while behind the scenes the liquor lobby that so graciously provided the meat gets a free pass for another year to peddle their poison to the community. And you'll hear no preaching from my father or any of his compatriots about self-control." She looked down at her feet, hoping he wouldn't challenge her on the hypocrisy, since she was still under the influence of the liquor lobby's product.

They approached the Monument in silence.

"It's the children who really suffer," Kitty said as they began to walk around the circle of flags at the base of the monument. She looked up at the stars, and then shifted her focus to the symbolic stripes of the fifty American flags that circled the path. Her companion abruptly stopped.

"You've been blessed."

"You're looking from the outside in," she muttered. Kitty sat down on one of the marble benches stationed around the circular path. "I can tell that you really believe in this stuff, that you can help people change."

He sat next to her and gave her a curious look.

Kitty turned her head and looked at the Monument. "When will you become like the others? How soon before you use the people's misery to line your own pockets? That's always what happens."

He cast her a sideways glance. "I can't believe how jaded you sound. Your father has remained true to the cause."

She hopped up and walked away. Me and my big mouth. She stopped in her tracks. What if he didn't follow? She smiled and reached out for his arm; he stood beside her. "We're not going to speak about him anymore tonight. It'll give me a headache, and I don't want that."

"Aren't you going to have a headache anyway?"

"Maybe, but not tonight."

They made another pass around the circle of flags in silence. Kitty stepped up on a marble bench and faced the Reflecting Pool. The dark waters shimmered in the slight night breeze. He stepped in front of her and obstructed her view of the Lincoln Memorial. She reached up and wrapped her arms around his neck. His large warm hands covered her waist.

She giggled as his mustache moved softly above her lips. "That tickles."

He pulled her closer and covered her mouth with a full, warm, deep kiss.

"My place or yours?" she asked breathlessly.

"Uh, no, Catherine, I don't think…"

"Call me Kitty." She pulled back, her brow creased. "Action, you're not married, are you? And don't lie to me, I don't do married."

Davis pulled her back into an embrace. "No, Kitty. I'm not married."

"Then how 'bout it?"

Davis stepped back, buried his hands deep into his pockets, and sat down on the cold marble and stared at the Reflecting Pool. She stood for a moment before joining him. He prayed the seats would cool them both down.

Davis warred with himself. Time, his rational mind reminded him, was the only known path back to sobriety. Maybe she wouldn't be so friendly when she was sober. His fingers wrapped around the condoms he'd taken from the restaurant's bathroom. They would provide no protection if he took unfair advantage of this situation. Congressman Franklin might be his childhood hero, but, more importantly, he was this lady's father. It wouldn't serve his best interest to anger the man.

He grinned. He'd never had an adventure like this before. He'd picked up a beautiful woman in a bar and was now on an impromptu date. Date?

Yes, this felt like a date, a first date and a good one. Sitting in the shelter of the Washington Monument on a stone bench with a soft thigh pressing against his was a fantasy for this former fat boy.

Kitty snuggled a little closer. It had been a while since his last relationship, but he wouldn't do it. But she is so petite and pretty, urged his penis, which he called Phat Head. Despite the cold seat, it was getting a little crowded in his pants. His rational mind responded, Are we actually considering letting a little twat ruin our chances of moving back home? Phat Head answered, Hell yeah!

It had been a long day. He was too tired to fight with himself any longer. He stood up. "Kitty, where do you live? I'd like to see you home."

"No." She poked her lips out. "I'm not ready to go. Can't we sit here for a few minutes? This is my spot. I come here and look up at the Monument to be reminded that my troubles aren't as large as they sometimes seem."

He sat back down and decided to join in with her philosophy. His reasonable side tried to warn him that spending more time with her would cause him an obelisk-sized problem. But there wasn't going to be a problem because he wasn't going to touch her. "Let me know when you're ready."

A park police officer came by at eleven-fifteen to inform them that he was going off duty. He hinted it might be a good time for them to leave. Davis stood up and stretched. Ahead of him the shadows of the homeless were moving towards their night resting spots. They couldn't have sat on that stone for more than ten minutes, but his butt ached. He kept one eye on Kitty while he asked for directions back to Union Station.

"Well, you can catch the orange line at the Smithsonian station...."

Davis narrowed his eyes and glanced at the slumped form on the bench.

The officer followed the direction of his gaze. "Maybe you should grab a cab across Fourteenth Street."

Kitty was barely coherent when he nudged and asked again about her address. The lateness of the hour and the alcohol had taken its toll. She struggled to open her eyes. "I'm not ready to leave you."

Chapter 3

"Ohh," Kitty moaned and shifted into the softness of a well-dressed bed. She was in a hotel room; she remembered strolling through the lobby a short while ago. She was torn between enjoying the comforts of the bed and the thoughts that raced through her brain. All her body wanted to do was give into the moment and relax further in this bed, but her brain kept up its processing logic. As she struggled, her eyes focused on the massive man that sat across from the bed on an easy chair.

"Secret Service protection?" She murmured as her brain clicked, again. "Secret Service protection doesn't mean you have to sleep in the chair."

"Huh?" his deep, sleepy voice moaned. "Yeah, Kitty, if you're ready I can take you home now."

"It's late, aren't you tired?" she said. "Come over here and lay down, make yourself comfortable."

He climbed into bed. Kitty moved close to him and kissed him. He wrapped his large hands around her and caressed her back. She toyed with the buttons on his shirt. "Umm. Do you have protection?"

He groaned and rolled over on his back. "We'd better stop. You're still a bit tipsy and I won't take advantage."

"I'm willing."

"No, we need to get up. Let me take you home now." He yawned.

His "no" sounded so resolute she was insulted. He'd rejected her. "I'm too tired to move," she pouted.

"I am, too." He yawned again.

"Then go to sleep," she snapped.

His eyes narrowed, then he shrugged his shoulders and rolled over on his side. Within seconds the grrr, grrr bellows of a bear-like growl filled the room.

Kitty sat straight up and blinked as her eyes adjusted to the dimly lit room. She opened the bedside table. The complimentary post card in the drawer was for the Washington Hilton. Now she had one of the answers her brain required. She peeped over the shoulder of the bear snoring contentedly on his side, hoping to answer the other. What was his name?

She crept out of bed, careful not to disturb him. Halfway to the bathroom, she looked back. He was dead to the world, knocked out. She should be mad instead of disappointed that he'd just rejected her. She shook her head in confusion. He was a rare man to stop. He'd actually told her no.

A few minutes later she stood fully dressed, listening to him snore. Her mind now on full alert, she realized she didn't know this man. She'd called him a Secret Service agent, but hadn't he told her something else? For the life of her she couldn't remember what. It was foolish for her to be here. But she didn't really want to leave. She was in no mood to negotiate getting home. And even in the middle of the night the DC spy system would still be hard at work. She didn't need to be seen leaving a hotel at this hour. For some strange reason she felt safe with him.

"What the hell?" She took off her shoes and slipped between the covers of the bed. She yawned, but sleep didn't come. Without knowing whether five minutes or five hours had passed, she gave up. Kitty sat up in the bed and pulled her knees to her chest. Her brain was wide awake. The memories from her day kept sleep at bay.

The morning had been very pleasant, shopping with her sisters, Yvette and Dena. She'd found the most perfect boots, and they hadn't argued once. Shortly after noon they'd returned to their parents' home and Kitty had excused herself to their father's study. She needed to check on the last-ditch legal maneuver she hoped would convince Linda McNair to drop the lawsuit. It had failed. But if her father's dumb luck held out, the press would wait until after Thanksgiving to run the story.

The argument began when she returned to the family room. In front of their mother and her six-year old niece, Quanice, Dena asked several off-limits questions. When Kitty refused to discuss the details of their father's legal affairs, citing attorney-client privilege, her older sister, Yvette, became enraged. Yvette got so angry she jumped out of her chair and walked around the room throwing her hands in the air and mumbling, "I can't believe this."

Kitty reached up and covered her mouth to stifle a laugh. Yvette was the ultimate drama queen. Her laugh faded as she remembered their mother's reaction. She'd watched their mother carefully during the exchange and, as usual, Yesenia had said nothing. They called her Yes behind her back because she never protested anything. True to form, during Yvette's outburst Yesenia had sat quietly, then rose and majestically left the room.

After their mother left, Kitty blessed her sisters out for bringing up their father's alleged infidelities. Yvette responded with bitter words, scolding Kitty for her loyalty to their father.

Kitty reached up and scratched her head. She wondered how much more her mother could take. This most recent affair was affecting them all more than the others.

Her thoughts went back to the end of the argument with her sisters. Not one to be verbally outmatched, Kitty put Yvette in check by questioning Yvette's faithfulness to Reggie, Quanny's non-child-support-paying father.

That shut 'Vette up.

"I should have stopped there," she whispered aloud. But she hadn't. She only meant to warn Dena. But the words didn't come out right. The timing wasn't right, either. She'd told Dena about a private detective's surveillance report she'd just received. Kitty would have sworn in court that her dark chocolate brown sister turned sheet white. With her sisters stunned into silence, she'd stormed out of the house.

She hadn't intended to stay at B Smiths' long, and she definitely hadn't meant to wind up in bed with a strange man. She glanced over at the snoring lump at her side and smiled. No, not a strange man; he was a rather pleasant person. Tall, dark, incredibly handsome, intelligent, articulate, fine, and kind. Her cheeks warmed as she remembered his gentle kisses at the Washington Monument. Chicago sisters must be out of their minds to let this one get away. She yawned and looked out the open drapes, catching a pre-dawn glimpse of the Washington Monument. A wave of comfort washed over her as she focused on the obelisk. She snuggled up against the agent's broad back.

Gentle fingers idly caressed Kitty's upper arm, lifting her out of a contented sleep. She purred and wiggled in closer.

"Kitty, you know you're safe here with me," his deep southern voice drawled.

"Uh-huh, I know you're Secret Service."

He chuckled, deep and throaty. "Why are you so fixated on the Secret Service?"

"I grew up with you guys, because of Daddy."

The caressing fingers stopped. "Wow, that's something I never considered."

Her ears perked. The tone in the agent's voice intrigued her. She stretched and yawned. The fog from sleep and her earlier activities had lifted. Her brain was now working as it should. "What?"

"As the child of a civil rights leader you probably had to endure a lot. Before now, I never considered what that might mean. No wonder you're well acquainted with the Secret Service."

She rubbed the spot on his chest where her hand lay. "We were never harmed, but threats were always present, especially in the eighties when there was so much racial legislation pending."

His fingers started again. "Ummm, like the fight over making Dr. King's birthday a national holiday?"

"No, I was thinking of the attempts by the Reagan administration to dismantle affirmative action." Kitty lifted her body and lay across the broad chest of her agent. His massive arms wrapped about her and he idly stroked her back. She lifted her head to look into his face. The stench of oxidizing alcohol filled her nostrils. "Ugh, I smell sour."

"A little sour." The agent gently pulled her forward and kissed the top of her head. "But overall I think you're sweet. If you want, you're welcome to take a shower. There's a hotel robe behind the bathroom door."

Kitty eyes widened.

"Don't worry, I'll walk down to the gift shop and get you a toothbrush."

What Southern kindness. This man was actually offering to leave his own hotel room so she could comfortably shower. "No, I'll just call the front desk and they'll bring one up." *What are you doing? Early morning light peeked through the window. If he was going to hurt me he could have done so last night.*

"Miss Kitty?" He nudged her.

"I'd love a shower, but why don't you go first?"

"Why, thank you, ma'am."

Kitty rolled over and watched as the massive man stood. She stifled a giggle when he placed his hands over his crotch to conceal his morning desires. She rolled over to the spot he'd vacated and inhaled, embracing the warmth his body left behind. "Oh, yeah." She took another deep breath of his manly scent and reached for the phone on the nightstand.

※

Feeling refreshed but a little shaky, Kitty stepped out of the hotel bathroom right into bright light. Pain filled her entire head.
"Would you like something to eat?"
She winced at the sound of his voice. "No, I think I'm going to be sick."
"Well, after last night…"
She held up her left hand, hoping he understood the universal sign to stop talking. Her right hand went to her forehead to shield her eyes from the sunlight. "Ohh!" It was time to get home. A little nauseous from the alcohol, she didn't need this throbbing in her head.
"Are you all right?" he asked. His voice was filled with concern.
"No. Where's my purse?"
Davis walked over to the sitting area, retrieved Kitty's handbag from the floor where she'd dropped it last night, and handed it to her. Then he closed the curtains. "You look like you need to lie down. Can I get you an aspirin or something?"
"No." She stumbled towards the bed. Bag in hand, she rummaged through it with the intensity of a big cat hunting prey. It took her a minute to find her quarry, a brown prescription bottle and her BlackBerry. Davis brought her a glass and the complimentary bottle of FIJI water.
"Can you open this?" She held the brown bottle aloft.
He sat next to her on the bed. "How many of these do you take?"
"I'd better start with three."
"You only have two left."
"Well, then give them to me," she snapped.
Her eyes opened long enough for him to hand her the pills. She gulped them down, then marched her fingers across the keyboard of her BlackBerry like an experienced Braille reader.
"It might still be a bit early to call someone. I'd be glad to see you home or try to get you wherever you need to go," he offered.

The lines around her eyes grew tighter, as if it hurt her to speak. "No. I'm calling Twanna." She bent her head and spoke into her phone. "I'm sorry, it's bad. I need my Reglan and…"

Her face twisted as she spoke to whoever was on the other end of her call.

"And a change of clothes. I'm at the Hinckley Hilton, room…What's the room number?"

He answered without being sure she was speaking to him. "Twenty-two-ten."

She continued without opening her eyes, "Yes, but no, not now. Room two-two-one-o. Please hurry."

Davis sat on the floor outside of room twenty-two-ten making his holiday phone calls. His long legs stretched well into the corridor. He had come out into the hall because he didn't want a sudden outburst to disturb Kitty. He needed to call his sister Jackie, who always made him laugh.

"Call Jackie." He waited while his voice-activated command connected with his younger sister. It had been two weeks since he'd talked to Captain Jackie Thornton, USAF, and she would have a dozen new adventures to share with him from her post in Korea.

After he filled Jackie in on his potential life changes and laughed at her adventures, he signed off and sat wondering if he'd made a direction-altering mistake. He shifted on the hard floor. He should go take advantage of the hotel's comfortable lobby. He stood up.

"Call home."

He chatted with his mother about some broken pickets in her fence and her arthritis, looking up every time he heard the ding of the elevator. He caught sight of a tall, slender woman dressed like an urban supermodel stepping from the elevator. The woman was dressed in form-fitting jeans, high-heeled fur-lined boots and a full-length blue jean jacket outlined in gold piping. She studied the hotel's directional signage, then headed towards him.

"Mama, I've got to go. I'll let you know later how everything works out."

The woman reached his side.

He stood.

"Twenty-two-ten?" she said with a lifted eyebrow.

Davis nodded. "Twanna?"

The woman gave him a total up-and-down assessment. As her eyes traveled lower, she grinned. "Where's she been hiding you?"

Self-conscious, he cupped his hands over his crotch. He was going to have to stop wearing these Nike Pro running tights.

"Are you one of Kitty's sisters?" In that moment he became hyper-aware of the situation. This could cause the congressman to change his mind about the job. It might have looked better if he had dressed for the day instead of wearing his workout gear. His plan for the day had been to take a run around the nation's capital before Thanksgiving dinner.

"No, I'm Twanna Matthews. And you are…?"

"Davis Thornton. Do you work in the congressman's office?"

"No, I work for Kitty. I'm her legal secretary/personal assistant. She didn't tell you about me?" Her smile widened as she took another look. "She didn't tell me about you, either. And I thought I knew all of her business."

Davis shrugged at her comment. Twanna seemed too much like the talky girlfriend type he liked to avoid.

"Okay, Mr. Too Fine. Where is she, and when did she catch the quake?"

Davis's lip twisted.

"The quake, that's what we call her headaches because of the sudden way they hit her."

"Early this morning."

He didn't care for the knowing look that crossed her skillfully made-up face. "Do you have her medicine?"

"Yes, I brought her things." Twanna's face softened with concern. "Is she asleep?"

Because of her expressed concern he altered his tone. "Yes, I just looked in on her."

"Good, then don't disturb her or she'll rip us both a new one. This gives us time to talk." Twanna stepped in a little closer and shifted from one foot to another. "This is Washington, you know how it works. Tell me something and I'll tell you something." She spoke in a conspiratorial tone. "How long have you been seeing Kitty?"

Davis shook his head in refusal. He wasn't from Washington, and he was not about to play this game.

"So you're not going to kiss and tell." Her eyes swept across his body again and landed on his face. "I can see why she didn't say anything to me, Big Fine. 'Cause she knows she's breaking our agreement. She usually goes for the shorter, skinnier guys and sends the big boys my way." Twanna winked.

Davis smiled and reconsidered while Twanna talked. There was something he wanted to know. "Does she do this kind of thing often?"

"What kind of thing?"

He was tempted to say 'get drunk and spend the night with a stranger.' His eyes narrowed as he looked over the Louis Vuitton train case and matching suit bag Twanna clutched. "Call you in the early morning to bring her a change of clothes?"

She took a step back. "No, she's a classy lady and doesn't work like that." Twanna lowered the travel luggage. It hit the floor with a thud. "But I do look out for her and she's really good to me. So if she needs me to bring her a suit to attend a last-minute event with her father—or for other reasons—I'm going to do it." She squared her shoulders and raised her head. Tall enough in her fur-lined boots, she looked him in the eye. "Now you tell me something. Are you man enough to deal with this or should I stay until she wakes up?"

Chapter 4

Kitty frowned as she looked at her watch. Five-thirty, just about time for her family to sit down for Thanksgiving dinner. She stared out the window of the white Lincoln Town Car she rode in with Action. A companionable silence filled the back seat as the driver sped through the uncharacteristically quiet streets of the District.

"What's on your mind?" he asked.

Her mind raced with questions and thoughts, but she bit her tongue to keep from saying the wrong thing. "I'm thinking about how incredibly nice you've been."

He grinned. "Miss Franklin, it's been an unexpected pleasure."

"You're nice to say that given the fact that I wasn't so pleasant earlier." She physically cringed when she recalled how she woke up shortly after noon and threw up all over the bathroom. Even through that, he'd been kind and understanding. She couldn't recall, but apparently they'd had a brief conversation during which she agreed to have dinner with him before she fell back asleep. When she woke up several hours later, she was curled up safely in his arms.

"It's all right. I'm just glad you're feeling better."

"For once I don't know what to say." She'd had boyfriends who demonstrated far less care for her than this man she had just met. She moved in a little closer. She craved more contact with this intimate stranger.

He put an arm around her shoulder. "You look very nice."

She looked into his eyes to accept his compliment. "Worth the wait?"

The only trace of impatience he'd shown with her was over the amount of time she'd taken to pull herself together for Thanksgiving dinner.

"I like you," she said.

The sides of his mustache turned up. "And I'm not quite sure why, Kitty Franklin, but I'd like to get to know you better."

Her cheeks burned as she looked down at her skirt. "Are you sure your friends won't mind me coming to dinner? Thanksgiving is such a family occasion."

He turned his face towards the opposite window. "Not at all. They'll love you."

It worried her not to remember where they were going. She wanted to say so, but her mouth had caused her enough trouble already. And she really wanted him to like her. Odds were it was someone she knew or should remember. The car crossed Military Road Northwest.

"Jackson?"

His head turned toward her. The corners of his mustache turned down. "You don't remember my name?"

She moved in even closer. "Yes, I do. It's Jackson Thornton, and that's not all I remember from last night."

"Ha, ha, ho." He drew his arm tightly around her waist and squeezed. "My name's Davis Thornton."

She bowed her head slightly. "Oops, sorry," she said as she tugged at his necktie. He allowed his head to bend until his mustache softly brushed her lips.

"That tickles." She giggled.

"That's what you said last night, when you kissed me at the Monument." He planted a dozen fine feather soft kisses around her lips before claiming his prize.

"That was unforgettable." Kitty drew in a deep breath and kissed him fully until they both gasped for air. She opened her eyes. Out the window she noticed the intersection of Western and Broad Branch roads. "Where are we going?"

"Kitty, our mothers attend the same church…."

She slid away from him on the seat.

"I told you, I'm from Rock Hill."

She scooted further away and looked out the window at very familiar scenery. "I asked you where we're going. And it's a rhetorical question." The car made a right on Aberfoyle Place.

Kitty clutched the door handle on her side of the back seat. "You lied to me."

"I don't lie."

The car rolled to a stop in front the federal style brick house where Kitty grew up. "Why didn't you tell me?"

"I tried. You kept stopping me."

"That's a weak defense. Daddy did send you. This whole thing, he probably set it up." She screamed and cradled her hands along the sides of her lowered head.

"No, ma'am. Now your father did suggest I have dinner last night at that restaurant, but he had no idea that I would meet you. That was truly a coincidence."

"I don't believe that. There are no coincidences, not in DC." She lifted her head, rolled her eyes, and loaded her tongue for a verbal assault. Her body shook. Loud and bitter, the words poured from her throat. "I don't know what kind of game you're playing, but I am not the one." She looked past him at the house. "If you think you'll curry favor with my father for bringing me home, you've wasted your time. I'm not going in there with you," she yelled.

His eyes widened. He reeled back from the force of her words. "Well, you might as well. You're yelling loud enough for the entire block to know you're out here."

"Go in there with you and say what?" she bit out.

"I'll tell your father the truth."

"And that is what? You picked his favorite daughter up drunk in a bar, spent the night with her."

"I've done nothing I'd be ashamed to say to your father."

She blinked back the hot tears that formed behind her lashes. *But I have.*

He reached a hand toward her. "I don't think it necessary to explain it all."

"Then you do lie."

His hand retracted from the fire in her accusation. The curbside door of the car opened and he slid over to step out.

"Driver," she scooted toward the open door. "Can you take me to Union Station?"

"Yes, ma'am," the driver responded over the top of the door he held open.

"Wait a minute," she yelled at Davis's retreating back. "My family never has guests for holidays. Daddy doesn't allow it. Who are you?"

Davis stood on the curb by the open car door. He bent down and peered in at Kitty. The way her arms waved rapidly reminded him of a hummingbird. If it wasn't for the force of gravity it looked as if she might take flight.

He turned around and leaned into the car's door frame. "I'm the new executive director of the Franklin Family Life Center."

"Damn it, Daddy," she yelled as her foot stomped down on the floorboards of the car. Another 'Dammit, Daddy,' escaped from the car's interior while he made arrangements with the driver to take Kitty wherever she needed to go and return to pick him up at 9 p.m.

"If she doesn't calm down, I'm not going to take her anywhere," the driver said loudly enough for her to hear.

The driver's protest was all he needed right now. Davis glanced into the car once more, then shut the door. He tipped the driver early and assured him she'd be okay. Davis took a deep breath. A cloud of uncertainty engulfed him as he walked toward the front door of Congressman Franklin's Washington home. He mouthed a quick prayer that Kitty wasn't planning a return trip to B. Smith's for a liquid holiday dinner. As he looked back at the Town Car pulling away from the curb, the front door of the house opened.

"Welcome, Davis."

Davis turned his head at the softness of Yesenia Franklin's voice.

"Come in, my boy," the congressman boomed.

As he stepped across the threshold, Mrs. Franklin greeted him by placing her hands on both of his arms. His muscles tightened.

"Relax," the older version of Kitty said as she released her soft grasp.

"Thank you, Mrs. Franklin."

"Now if you're going to put your feet under my table you must call me Yesenia."

"Yes, ma'am," he replied.

"Come on in and make yourself at home." The older man gave him a hearty slap on the back. He followed them into their home. This couple was a study in contrasts. The congressman was big, black, and burly while his wife was a light-skinned, petite, delicate-looking lady. An old adage ran through his mind. If true, he knew exactly how Kitty would look in the future.

"Excuse me, I need to get back to my kitchen." Yesenia stepped away.

"Come on into the family room and meet the rest of my family." Roosevelt Franklin stepped out of the foyer and motioned for Davis to follow. "We're all here except for my middle daughter, Catherine."

A tinge of remorse gripped his chest as he followed his host into the family room. He'd imagined there would be lots of people to meet today. He wasn't quite prepared for a family dinner.

"Davis, these are my daughters, Yvette and Dena, my granddaughter, Quanice, and Quanny's father, Reggie." Roosevelt pointed to and named everyone waiting in the den. Kitty had been right; Thanksgiving at the Franklins' was strictly a family affair.

He sat down by Dena on the sofa and observed the incomplete family portrait. Genetics was indeed a strange subject. The oldest daughter, Yvette, favored the mother, but not to the same degree as Kitty. The congressman's genes dominated Dena. She was taller and darker than her sisters. And Dena had the strong facial features of her father. Though she lacked facial beauty, the gene pool had compensated her with a bombshell of a figure.

He participated in the light conversation and answered all of Yvette's probing questions about his background. His ears burned at each mention of Kitty. He really should speak up. Her family was waiting dinner just for her. Was Kitty's indictment true? Was he a liar for not telling her family what he knew? He squirmed a bit in his seat when Yvette asked him if he was married or had any children.

"Now you know that's none of your business," Dena said and shot a look at her sister.

Before he could respond Yesenia Franklin re-entered the room. She walked gracefully over to her husband and touched his arm. "Rosey, I'll serve dinner now. Kitty just called. She won't be joining us."

His breath caught at the sound of Yesenia's voice. Her soft tone sounded very much like Kitty's when… Well, how Kitty sounded when she wasn't angry.

The congressman stood and towered over his wife. "And you just let her get away with that?" The displeasure in his voice quieted the room. Guilty glances passed between the sisters.

"Rosey, please, we have guests," Yesenia said.

"Fine by me," Yvette let out.

"At least she called, Daddy," Dena offered.

Davis drew in a sharp breath.

After a long second of silence, Roosevelt waved his arm over his head. "Y'all heard the lady. Dinner is served."

After dinner Davis joined the congressman for a private discussion in the study. The room's aged leather chairs combined with the essence of cigar to create an atmosphere of masculine influence and power. Dreading the discussion, Davis stood and looked out the window. He wondered where Kitty had gone.

"My girls are great, but Kitty's the one I needed you to meet. She didn't give me any sons, so I had to take one of her daughters. And I tell you, I couldn't ask for a finer son than my Kitten."

A lump formed in Davis's throat. Now was probably a good time to come clean. "Sir, I already know your daughter."

"Fine, that's fine."

Davis looked into the darkness as Roosevelt sang the praises of his special girl. According to her father, Kitty was bright and effective. "She's a damn fine lawyer, as good as they come." The congressman glowed as he praised her.

Kitty was correct. He couldn't tell him where she'd spent the night. How could he tell this father how he'd met his favorite daughter?

Instead of speaking up, Davis turned his attention to the bookcase-lined walls while Roosevelt poured after-dinner cognac. The shelves were a shrine to the congressman's accomplishments, with pictures of Roosevelt Franklin with every significant figure of the past two decades, presidents and politicians, celebrities and world leaders.

He'd had a remarkable career, despite a somewhat controversial beginning. Roosevelt Franklin was supposed to be a participant in the most famous civil rights protest in their hometown of Rock Hill. But for some reason Franklin hadn't shown up on the day the Rock Hill Nine made history. He'd spent several years as a community organizer before a long term in the U.S. Congress. Davis had patterned his own career of community service after Franklin's example.

He moved away from the bookshelves to accept his drink. "Isn't Reggie joining us?"

"No, only men are invited into my study. Yesenia's free to invite him for the holiday, but not in here. This is my domain."

Davis took a sip to mask his expression. His host had just dissed Dr. Reginald Ward, his granddaughter's father and a third-year resident at the prestigious Boston General Hospital.

"Son, any fool can make a baby. It takes a man to raise a child." He raised his glass in mock salute. "You did answer truthfully to all of the interview questions? If you didn't, Kitty's got a crack team of investigators, and she will find out."

"Yes, sir, I don't lie. I don't have any children." This was the second time today he'd asserted his veracity to a member of this family. He could hear his mentor's voice in his ear reminding him that there were lies of commission and lies of omission.

"I like the way you answered that. Can't stand to hear a fool say 'not that I know of.' A man knows whether or not he's fathered a child. And a man always provides. Reason enough for a man to work. To provide for his family, not resolve his intellectual curiosity." Another slam against Dr. Ward. The older man moved to sit behind his polished mahogany desk. "Yesenia is very fond of you. I'd hate to disappoint her."

Davis took another sip and moved to occupy one of the dark leather wingback chairs that faced the desk. As he settled into the well-conditioned leather he had the distinct feeling he'd become a part of some political or personal maneuver. Kitty had said there were no coincidences in DC. "Mrs. Franklin is a kind and gracious lady. I'm grateful she remembered me."

"She couldn't stop talking about you after she heard you speak this spring at the church. I'm glad you were open to discuss the opportunity to become director at the Center." Roosevelt raised his glass. "Here's hoping everything checks out so I can remain in Yesenia's good graces."

As he held his glass aloft for the toast, Davis regretted the mistake he'd made with Kitty. All he could do now was hope she'd be gracious enough to speak with him again.

Kitty turned over a dry turkey sandwich and the pages of Davis Thornton's dossier for the fifth time. The hungrier she got for her mother's home-cooked meal the angrier she became at her big undisciplined mouth. Why hadn't she just gone into the house for dinner with Davis Thornton?

He seemed to be the finest, nicest, most decent man she'd met in years. Unlike most men, instead of taking advantage, he'd taken care of her. She wrapped her arms around her frame and remembered the warmth of lying in his arms. His credentials claimed he was a powerful motivational speaker, but his tone with her had been soft and reassuring. She'd believed him when he told her she was safe.

His education seemed disjointed. A bachelor's in political science and two master's degrees, one in social work and another in theology. When she reviewed his work history, it made sense. He'd spent his career working for various church, civil rights and human rights groups. His current job in Chicago was as a grants manager for a private philanthropic organization. His references called him competent. But all she knew was he was caring. During the short time she'd spent with him she'd felt safe, cherished, and loved.

Maybe if he'd told her they were going to her parents' house for dinner, things would be different. But maybe he had and she didn't remember. She recalled how her brain hadn't functioned well last night. Instead of picking at a dry sandwich she could be enjoying a slice of her mother's famous coconut cream pie. She picked up her plate and walked to her kitchen. Kitty glanced over at the microwave oven. Nine-twenty. She grinned. By now she would have figured out a way to leave the house with Davis and they could have finished what was started earlier in the back seat of that Town Car.

She leaned against the granite counter, closed her eyes, and sighed. His kisses still warmed her, and remembering the brush of his mustache against her lips caused a thrill to tickle her spine. Her knees buckled and her pink-bunny-slipper-clad feet slipped out from under her. She caught the edge of the counter before she hit the floor.

"Don't be so stupid, you're tired, not weak in the knees. He hasn't swept you off your feet. This isn't a fairy tale." She walked back to her desk, grinning.

She flipped though his squeaky clean background check again. Professionally everything was in order, and personally, no marriages, no baby mamas, no arrests or other drama. "If a man could sweep me off my feet it might be you, Davis Thornton," she said to the manila file as she wrote down her recommendation. She stuffed the file into her briefcase and then pulled out a sheet of her personal stationary to thank Davis Thornton for his kindness. She wrote him a thank-you note, just as her mother had taught her.

He probably wouldn't want to have anything to do with her. Not after the way she'd acted earlier. "Me and my big mouth," Kitty yelled to her pen as she spelled out the address to his office in Chicago. She sealed the envelope, reached for her BlackBerry, and pressed her father's private number.

Chapter 5

The next morning, from her perch in the window seat of her father's study, Kitty stared in the direction of the capitol. She continued second-guessing all the decisions she'd made yesterday. She was right not to walk into this house with Davis Thornton for Thanksgiving dinner. But she was wrong for being so mean to such a nice man. But recommending against his hire? Was that the right thing to do? Her eyes strained upward in search of the obelisk. The glimpse of the Washington Monument she needed couldn't be found from here. If Daddy hadn't demanded she wait here, she'd go upstairs and sit in the window seat of her room to think. From her window she could see the Monument.

The point of reference in her life for as long as she could remember had been the Monument. It gave her perspective every time things seemed impossible. Its towering presence over the city reassured her that there were answers, even to her father's legal and moral problems. Her mother and grandmother had God; she'd decided to believe in the Monument. It never failed to give her a sense of peace.

Kitty turned at the sound of her father's deep bass voice. She hopped up and scurried toward the men at the door.

Her father stepped toward her. "I believe you know Davis Thornton."

She moved around him and stopped in front of her handsome good Samaritan. "I'm sorry," she blurted out.

"I'm glad to hear that," Davis said.

"Sorry for what?" Roosevelt said to her back.

She turned her head and glared at her father. "Daddy, will you excuse us for a minute," she said sweetly.

"Kitty, you know I can't stand it when you take that tone with me." The congressman cast a sideways glance at his guest. "She's the spitting image of her mother, and when she takes that tone she knows she sounds just like her mother and so I can't refuse her." Roosevelt threw up his hands in defeat. With a furrowed brow he looked from Davis to his daughter and back again. He took two steps to the door and paused with his hand on the door knob. "Uh, how well do you know him?"

"That doesn't concern you." Kitty moved over to her father and gave him a little shove.

"Yesenia," he yelled as she shut the door.

She returned to a smiling Davis.

"You were right. I should have insisted on telling you everything," he said.

Her eyes roamed his broad chest. "It's okay. I hope we can still be friends."

His mustache quivered. "Friends?"

"Yes?"

"Kitty, I meant what I said yesterday. I want to get to know you better."

She reached her arms up as a broad smile covered her face. "You do?"

He bent and touched her lips with his. "How tall are you?"

"Five three, why do you ask?"

He looked down at her feet. "Without shoes?"

Kitty cast her eyes toward her high heeled boots. "Four eleven," she said with a sheepish grin as she stepped up on her toes.

He straightened and stretched his back. "What is it about you, girl?"

Kitty grinned from ear to ear. She reached up and wrapped her arms around his waist. The warm safety of embracing him took away all of her frets. When the door knob clicked, her eyes flew open.

"Kitty, what are you doing? Oooh, I'm gonna tell Daddy." Her younger sister Dena hurriedly stepped inside the office and closed the door behind her. She stood with her hands hugging her wide hips like a fishwife with fresh gossip.

Kitty stepped away from Davis's embrace to square off with her sister. "You aren't going to tell Daddy anything." She held her hand up to stop Dena from speaking. "And if you do, I'll give him that surveillance report about you."

Dena rolled her eyes and took a step back. She crossed her arms over her chest. "You're going to give it to him anyway."

"Yes, I am. But I was going to wait until Monday when you're safely back at school."

Davis stood between the sisters. "I'll speak to your father about us."

"No." Kitty's brow furrowed as she looked from a frowning Davis to her sister. "Neither one of you has anything you need to tell him."

A short time later Davis sat in a captain's chair aboard the smartly outfitted tour bus set to serve as the congressman's mobile campaign office. Now he'd become a participant in a campaign strategy meeting. He leaned back into the stiff white leather seat. It was nice, but not nearly as comfortable as the well-worn leather chairs in the congressman's study. Davis crossed his arms and shifted in the seat. He curled his index finger above his lip to contain the smile that kept creeping onto his face. He was tickled and a bit in awe of the professionalism Attorney Catherine Franklin displayed as she led her family through a series of campaign decisions. She was so different from any woman who'd ever showed him any attention before he lost a hundred pounds.

"So we agree on logo five, the blue banner with red stars?" Kitty was trying to put an end to an issue they'd tried to resolve for the past fifty miles. In his wildest dreams he'd never imagined spending this day en route to Cape May, New Jersey, engaged in a protracted discussion about the impact a simple logo might have on Congressman Franklin's bid for re-election.

He was supposed to be on a plane to Chicago this morning, but Roosevelt had insisted he stay over one more day and meet with Kitty. The congressman had implied that it would be well worth his while, so he'd changed his flight this morning. He'd spent most of the night ruminating over the opportunity he'd missed to tell the truth after dinner last night. He stretched his long legs out. Travel fatigue, plus worry over Dena's discovery, gnawed at him. Is Kitty worth risking so much? his rational mind demanded.

"Davis, what do you think?" The sweet voice of Yesenia Franklin lifted him from his thoughts.

Kitty jumped in. "He doesn't live in the District."

"He will by the election," Yesenia answered.

Kitty stumbled, although the bus hadn't hit a bump.

"I don't think I should comment," Davis replied.

"You're a voter, right?" Roosevelt, seated opposite him in a matching chair, made his first comments of the entire trip.

"Yes, sir, every election."

"Then we want to know," he said.

Urged on by the candidate, Davis gave his input on the proposed logos while Kitty sat stone-faced on a high chair. For the rest of the trip she seemed a bit off her game. She kept relatively quiet, just saying what was necessary to conclude the business. Every few miles she'd look his way and give a shy smile. Then he'd glance over at Dena, who was still wearing her I'm-going-to-tell-it smirk. Dena winked. He sank down deeper into his seat.

○○○

Two hours later Davis sat with the Franklins on the wraparound porch of the family's country cottage. The beauty of the manicured lawns and maple trees surrounding the family house reminded him why he wanted so badly to move home. And he couldn't keep his eyes off Kitty. The expression on her face was priceless. She glowed in delight as she ate the coconut cream pie her mother had brought just for her. Kitty was quiet as she ate, and the conversation developed without her.

"There aren't any decent young men out there for you girls," Roosevelt said. "It's a damn shame what has happened to this generation of black men." Roosevelt rocked in his Adirondack chair. "Rappin', ruggin', or thuggin'. Not good enough for my girls." Roosevelt cut his eyes at Dr. Reggie.

Davis held his breath and wondered what Roosevelt thought about him.

"Maybe by the time Quanny comes of age, like around thirty, black men will be worth a damn again."

"Don't start, Rosey." Yesenia patted Quanice's arm and pointed the child towards the lawn. The little girl hopped up and ran into the yard.

"What about your new friend here, Daddy?" Dena walked over to their father and wrapped her long arms around his neck from behind. "You were going on and on last night about what a fine young man he is."

Kitty turned in a flash and huffed, "Shut up, Dena."

Davis's eyebrow shot up. He glanced around at everyone. The mood on the porch shifted. Reggie and Yvette seemed very uncomfortable; they both shifted in their chairs.

"Davis is a fine young man." Yesenia stood and went into the house.

"Reggie, why don't you tell us what you've been working on," Yvette stammered out in an attempt to change the direction of the conversation. "I've been doing some research on the effects of rap music on the level of cortisol in the body and how that contributes to violence." Reggie shone as he talked about his research. He bored them with scientific data about chemicals and hormones for several minutes.

Kitty stretched and stood. "You do any research into what hormone is needed to get a brother to pay child support?"

Davis leaned back in the rocker. Kitty hit hard and drove deep. He'd experienced that yesterday.

"Why don't you shut up?" Yvette shrieked. "Your mouth is why you don't have a man." Yvette reached over to Reggie and took his arm. "I'm sorry, Reggie, but you know how she is. Let's go play with Quanny." The couple stepped off the porch and called to their daughter.

Kitty cut her eyes at a grinning Dena and set her plate on the porch rail. "I'm going for a walk." She stepped off the porch and moved quickly around the side of the house.

Dena smirked at Davis, then slammed the door on her way into the house.

In less than a minute the porch had cleared. "Okay if I check out your grounds?" he half asked Franklin before stepping into the yard. He followed in Kitty's direction. It didn't take many of his long-legged strides to catch up with her on a path lined with what looked like Carolina pine trees. He inhaled. The scent reminded him of home.

"Wait up, Kitty."

She stopped in her tracks and swung around. "What took you so long?"

"I had to wait a respectable amount of time." He winked. "I didn't want to be talked about."

"I'm sorry about that. It usually happens when my family gets together." She sucked in her lower lip and kicked a rock. She looked back toward him. "Somebody needed to say it," she started, defending her actions. "Reggie hasn't paid a dime in child support since he began medical school. He doesn't come from money and he's struggling to achieve his dreams, but it isn't fair. The strain of being a single parent is really aging my sister. I just hate to see her and Quanny suffer. I shouldn't have opened my big mouth, but—" She took a few steps along the path.

He fell in step and they walked along the path toward a tool shed. She stopped in front of the small building and leaned up against it. Her head hung low. Davis put his arm on the wall and leaned in close. His mustache brushed her face as he planted a kiss on her cheek. "I like your mouth." He enveloped her mouth in a warm kiss, stopped, then kissed her again. "I like your mouth like this."

"What? Closed?"

Davis chuckled. "Not quite." Davis slid his tongue between her parted lips and claimed another kiss. His hands roamed down and cupped her breast.

"What the hell?"

Kitty startled at her father's voice. Davis stepped back.

"Uh, sir, I can…"

"Daddy?"

"Don't 'Daddy' me. What the hell's going on out here?"

Davis stood in front of Kitty. "Sir, I think I should explain."

She put her hands on his back and nudged him aside, then she took two steps toward her father. It looked like a house cat preparing to charge a lion. "Daddy, this isn't any of your business."

The lion of congress took a step back.

"Young man, go back to the house and say your goodbyes. The driver is ready to take you and Reggie back to the city anyway. I came out here to get you, not to find you up in my daughter's face like this."

"Daddy, please," Kitty roared.

Roosevelt marched to the door of his shed. "I want you and Reggie both away from here now so I can spend the weekend with my girls." With a murderous expression he stepped over the threshold and slammed the door.

How dare you and *hypocrite* sat on the tip of her tongue. Kitty pulled in her lower lip to keep words in her mouth.

"He doesn't have any tools in there, does he?" Davis asked, half in jest. The man had just caught him feeling up his favorite daughter.

"No, just the tools of his trade, a cell phone, computer, fax machine, machete. We better get out of here." Kitty grinned and grabbed Davis's hand to lead him up the path to the main house.

Fifteen minutes later Kitty stood with her mother and Yvette as the campaign bus carried Davis and Reggie away from the farm. She lifted her arm and waved. She should have gone with him. He'd asked. But she'd already committed to spending the weekend with her parents. It was rare for her family to spend an entire weekend together. She'd already missed Thanksgiving dinner and there was work to do with Daddy. She also wanted to be near Yvette. From the look on her face Reggie had finally summoned the courage to drop his big news on her. She lowered her arm as the bus rounded the bend.

She turned toward her sister. "Want to talk about it?"

Yvette took two steps backward. "How the hell did you know?" she shrieked.

"Daddy," Kitty said.

"He had him investigated and you read the report. He puts a tail on Dena and you hold the report." Yvette placed her hands on her hips. "I hate it when you do this kind of stuff. I know you and Daddy are thick as thieves, but this is me. You should have told me."

"It wasn't her place," Yesenia said.

Yvette's eyes widened. She shrieked again and ran toward the house.

Despite her reputation for having a big mouth, Kitty could be the soul of discretion. She'd known for months that Reggie was engaged to a fellow resident at Boston General. She'd often wondered when Reggie was going to tell Yvette. And even though she was roiling mad about the reportedly extravagant wedding plans, she'd held her tongue. That wasn't any of her business. But when the time was right she'd make sure Yvette filed for court-ordered child support. Even if Reggie did have a boatload of student loan debt, she vowed to make sure he paid his fair share to support Quanny. Kitty looked down the road in the direction of the campaign bus. "Shoot, he doesn't have my number."

"But you have his," her mother said.

She whipped around to face her mother. She'd almost forgotten her mother was still standing next to her. "How do you know?"

"Your father asked me before we left the house how you knew him and Dena told on you before we left."

Her mouth flew open. "She didn't tell Daddy?"

"No, but you should have known she wouldn't keep it. This is the first thing she's had on you in years. I've been watching you both all day."

Kitty huffed.

Yesenia's shoulders slumped. "Kitty, please let this thing with Dena go until Monday, like you said you would. I've already got Yvette to take care of, and I'd like some peace this weekend."

She looked into her mother's weary eyes. "Okay, but…"

"What, Kitty?" she whispered.

She looked out to the horizon. "Nothing." No reason to ask a question that wouldn't get answered. Her mother wouldn't have anything to say about Davis or Reggie. She never gave opinions on their relationships and rarely gave her daughters dating advice. For this, and the nonsense she took from their father, Kitty and her sisters thought their mother was weak.

"Catherine, a relationship is between two people."

Had Yesenia spoken? Or was she just conceptualizing their mother's oft-repeated mantra?

Kitty watched her mother's slow pace. Was she tired from the holiday cooking? Or saddened by Daddy's most recent infidelity? Or just getting old? She reached up and rubbed her temples. Hell, dealing with Daddy's mess was aging her, too. Her cell phone chirped. She rolled her eyes and reached into her pocket. "What now?" She scrolled to read a text message.

GET DOWN HERE NOW.

She trudged off in the direction of her father's shed.

Chapter 6

Kitty tapped on the mahogany desk in her father's Rock Hill office. She sat back, engulfed in the massive wing chair. Her eyes roamed the office. Her father was so predictable. This place was just the same as his Washington dugout. Too many times in the past year when a headache assaulted her, she'd had a hard time remembering where she was when she worked from his offices. Her eyes stopped at her luggage. Not today. She was in Rock Hill, and so was Davis.

A butterfly fluttered in her stomach. Should she take the weekend off when she was so far behind in her work? Especially with a new task of media monitoring on her plate? When her father asked her to take this on during the Thanksgiving weekend she'd never imagined it would be so time consuming. The twenty-four-hour news cycle required almost constant surveillance for websites and blogs where unfavorable information and unflattering opinion might be posted.

This was a problem for her father. In the cyber world, public opinion had turned against the old guard of the civil rights establishment. The people, or rather cyber society, questioned the lack of progress for the movement. Forty years after Doctor King, what had been accomplished, outside of an impressive array of elected officials and high ranking corporate officers?

Media monitoring seemed more like a prurient distraction than actual work. The sites churned more on salacious gossip about marital infidelities and financial scandals than serious inquiry about why the movement seemed stalled. Next week she'd hire someone to manage this.

She keyed in one particular site. The blog stood dangerously close to her serving notice to the service provider for breach of terms of service. It was dedicated solely to the foibles of Roosevelt Franklin. She suspected the blog was owned by her father's opponent in the upcoming primary election, but she couldn't prove it yet. The site had some sophisticated programming, and knowing his uneducated opponent she feared the site was bankrolled by some third-party threat. *Great, nothing new posted so far today.*

She pushed back from the desk. In all honesty, media monitoring wasn't the real reason she was behind. Too much of her time in the past two weeks had been spent online and on the phone with Davis. She'd called him late on the Friday night after Thanksgiving, as soon as she finished fighting with her father. Her father had actually tried to chastise her for kissing Davis.

Davis called her back as soon as he arrived in Chicago. They'd communicated constantly ever since. Her conscience kicked her every time they talked. Davis was just too good a man to be caught up in her father's web of lies and political machinations.

She pulled the chair back toward the keyboard to type out a last email to Twanna, final instructions for closing the case file on Linda McNair. It had taken quite a bit more money and a cushy job with the South Carolina Secretary of State's office, but she'd done it again for Daddy.

"The unrepentant liar," she blurted out.

Kitty believed every word of Linda's story and the blog post about how the affair began and ended. But as his daughter she did what she must to protect the family's greatest asset: her father's name.

As soon as the press conference to introduce the new director of the Center was over, she was out of there. Kitty frowned and tugged at the ends of her hair. Her father had deliberately kept her out of the loop in the hiring of the new director by assigning her this media mess and focusing her attention on the McNair business.

Kitty slammed her laptop shut. She shuddered as she remembered the bitter argument she'd had with her father at the farm over her recommendation not to hire Davis. It had been the last conversation they'd had about the Center. She didn't know who he'd hired and she didn't really care. She only knew her mother insisted it not be a woman.

Her father considered the Franklin Family Life Center the crowning achievement of his political career. He'd established the center with taxpayer dollars, corporate sponsorships, and private foundation money. How he managed to use his congressional budget to pay rent in the building he owned was just one of his Houdini-like tricks.

In addition to the congressman's district offices, the Center housed a banquet hall, meeting rooms, a day care center, and a gym. Local civic organizations and all the African-American sororities and fraternities rented space to hold their monthly meetings. The Center's banquet hall made a ton of money each year by hosting cotillions, fashion shows, and other fundraisers.

Her father's other great trick was to underwrite the Center's operating budget through a yearly congressional appropriation. Then he charged the government rent when the space was used for after-school tutoring and the summer youth employment program. And the money they made staying open late for the federally funded midnight basketball league was astronomical.

Kitty chewed on her lower lip. With his background, Davis would have been excellent at managing all of this. Maybe she was wrong for asking her father not to hire him.

She was at the happy start of a relationship with the kind, generous man who'd rescued her on Thanksgiving. She'd been too busy working out the McNair affair and media mess to run to Chicago and spend every weekend with him, as she wanted to. And Davis said he was swamped with his work in Chicago, so he couldn't make a return trip to DC. But they made do, communicating via the phone and computer. Any time the Franklin Center came up in conversation she skirted the issue, until last week when he wouldn't let her dodge his questions about the annual Christmas party.

Davis had been contracted as a guest speaker in May, something else she knew nothing about. Kitty knew ninety percent of her father's secrets; the other ten percent she found out when he was in trouble. Davis had asked if she would attend as his date.

"...only if you'll stay the weekend," she remembered saying.

He called her the most forward girl he'd ever met and reminded her how much he liked it.

Kitty grinned and walked toward the office door. "Davis, you're too good to be true."

For the first time in years she had a date this weekend for her father's annual thank-you to all of the people who worked the political campaigns and supported the Center. Folks in Rock Hill considered it the social event of the holiday season. It was a 'big get' to receive the hand-engraved invitation.

She checked her watch as she quickly stepped through the halls of the Franklin Center. All she had to do was make sure nothing went astray at this press conference, then call Davis and be on her way. She stopped short of the ballroom door. A tingle of excitement shot up her spine. *I wonder if he's already in town.*

She strolled confidently into the multi-purpose room set up for the conference. As she made her way to the front she said hello to several cousins and family friends. Her father was generous with his favors. He would find or make a job for anyone that claimed kinship, through birth or political support. She took a chair on the front row next to her grandmother, Catherine Franklin.

"Hey, Mama Cat."

"Hey, baby."

At eighty-seven, Mama Cat's body was frail, but her mind was still sharp as a tack.

"Kitty Kat, your smile is as bright as the Carolina sunshine," Mama Cat said. "I hope to meet your young man soon. Your mother went on so about him after he spoke at that church of hers, I almost regretted not going." Mama Cat was slow to forgive, and she never forgot. She still held a grudge against the Baptist Methodist Assembly Church for holding organizing meetings during the civil rights era. It was at those meetings that the Rock Hill Nine made their plans and where her son had met the little slip of a girl from the east he'd married. "I'm mad at you anyway. We haven't had much of a visit. You spent all day yesterday on that computer or talking on that cell phone."

Kitty reached over and gave her grandmother a one-armed hug. "No, I didn't. We had a good long talk last night and you got all up in my business. I can't wait for you to meet Davis tomorrow night."

The older woman looked toward the door. "Will it be that long?"

Kitty shifted her attention to the stage. She needed to get her mind on her job. Before she could reach behind her to pick up a briefing package, her cousin Glynnis sashayed out of the side door and up to the podium. Glynnis worked in various capacities at the Center and served as the congressman's southern press secretary.

"May I have y'all's attention," Glynnis warbled. She always sounded as if she had marbles in her mouth.

Kitty cringed at Glyn's grammar and outfit. Today she sported a Farrah Fawcett blonde wig or weave, with a tight fitting, short-skirted, leopard-print business suit. Still looking foolish at forty.

"We's beginning in five minutes. Any background information that y'all needs is in them folders on the chairs. There will be two announcements, followed by a brief statement. And the congressman will not be taking any questions."

Yesenia Franklin slid into the seat next to her daughter and whispered loud enough for Kitty and Mama Cat to hear, "She looks ridiculous." All three Franklin women stifled a grin as the side door opened and Roosevelt Franklin strode in, followed by Davis Thornton. Davis winked when he caught her eye as they walked in. She smiled, a reflex.

Five minutes later Kitty still furiously tapped her foot. She should have seen this coming a mile away. How could she have missed this? Her father had duped her. Why hadn't Davis told her? Now she couldn't look at him. She hung her head and listened as her father rained down compliments and accolades on the new director of the Franklin Family Life Center.

A bony elbow struck her rib cage. She turned toward her grandmother.

"That's a fine looking man."

Kitty's heart leaped in her chest. She had to look up. Davis now stood at the podium waiting for a burst of applause to die down.

"Calm down, Kitty," her mother whispered.

Her foot stopped. She looked on either side of her at the two women who were polar opposites but thick as thieves. Then she cut her eyes at her father. It was a classic wag-the-dog maneuver. He got her all involved in media monitoring while he hired Davis against her counsel. But why? Daddy usually took her legal advice. As angry as she was with her father, it didn't approach the intensity of her fury with Davis. Her legs shook. He should have told her. She turned her head to get a look at the Thornton family sitting across the aisle. The lot of them beamed with pride. Well, in all fairness, if Davis had told her she would have intervened and they wouldn't be here.

She returned to staring at her wobbly knees.

"Don't be too angry, Kitty," her mother said. But her legs wouldn't settle. She placed her hands under her thighs to stop her heels from clicking on the floor. She sneered at her mother, then looked back up at the stage. Davis was in mid-sentence about his plans for the Center. He caught her eye and vocally stumbled.

Before Davis could sit down one of the reporters from the Daily Herald jumped to his feet.

"Congressman Franklin, care to clear up the reports concerning the previous director's departure?"

Roosevelt Franklin shook his head. "No."

A local television reporter pushed a fuzzy black microphone forward.

"What about the sexual harassment suit? Or the rumors about a love child?"

"No comment." Roosevelt Franklin rose and motioned to Kitty to get on post.

Kitty rolled her eyes and stood to face the audience. "I'm Catherine Franklin, the congressman's attorney. I'll ask that you respect the presence of my mother, Yesenia Franklin, and my grandmother, the congressman's eighty-seven-year-old mother. We are here today to announce the appointment of Mr. Thornton. That being accomplished, this meeting is over."

Kitty turned and lifted the brakes of her grandmother's wheel chair as the dais party left the room. Yesenia followed. Once in the holding room, Kitty gave her grandmother a hasty goodbye. With steam pouring out of her ears she barreled toward Davis. His smile faded as she closed in.

"Kitty, will you join me in my office? Please?" He placed his hand on the small of her back and guided her from the holding room. Her spine stiffened and her heels clicked angrily across the laminate floors as they crossed the hall.

After he closed the door to the private office, Kitty folded her arms across her heaving chest. With an icy gaze she unloaded her tongue.

"That's all you got for the man who's thought about nothing but you for the past two weeks?"

She shifted her stance and rested her hands on her hips. "It's seems to me that you had a few other things on your mind." She drew in a sharp, angry breath and studied his expression.

His lids were half closed and his arms were folded tightly across his chest. His eyes narrowed. "Kitty," he growled.

Yvette's warning from the farm leaped into her brain. Don't you dare say another word. She skittered across the floor and threw herself in his arms.

Davis received her with wide open arms and lifted her face for his kiss.

"Ummm," he moaned. "That's what I'm talking about."

She pushed back and stepped away from his embrace. "You lied to me." Just can't keep it closed, can you?

He took a step toward her. "I admit, I omitted…"

"Oh, no. See, you're already corrupted. You admit you omitted? Did you learn that from my father? Why the hell didn't you tell me?"

"Because your father threatened to fire me before I started if I breathed a word of this to you." His mustache turned down.

Her shoulders lowered. This was exactly what she was afraid of. "See how he works?"

As she remembered how it felt to be consistently outmaneuvered by the master manipulator, the last vestiges of her anger melted. She stretched her arms out. He covered the distance between them in one of his giant steps. Kitty wound her arms tightly around him. "Davis, you're too good a man to get caught up in this."

"Thank you, Kitty, I'm glad you think that. But you had to know how much I wanted this job and…" He stepped back and folded his arms in front of his chest. "I had already put this opportunity at risk more than you'll ever know. I need to be back in Rock Hill to help out my mother. Jackie's in Korea, Sharon's wanting to start her family, my father's gone. It's time for me to step up."

"I can understand why you didn't tell me. But I still feel like you've been lying to me all this time," she said flatly.

"I know, and I promise if you forgive me this will be the last lie between us told by me. You don't know how hard this has been for me. How I wanted to share this with you. I like what's developing between us, and it ate me up knowing I was putting it at risk."

Kitty looked down at her shoes. She was a liar, too. Maybe now would be a good time to tell him she'd recommended against his hiring.

Davis reached for her and wrapped her in his arms.

That could wait.

"Kitty, I'm a grown man. Trust that I can handle my business."

"Okay, but be careful."

"That's all you got for your man? Be careful?" He held her back a bit and grinned. "Not even begrudged congratulations?"

She wrapped her arms around his waist, inhaled his scent, and squeezed her body closer to his. "I've been looking forward to standing right here for two weeks."

He bent down and kissed her face, then straightened. "That's better than congratulations. Let's sit down on the sofa before I hurt my back."

Arm-in-arm, they walked to the sofa in his office.

Ever forward, Kitty climbed into his lap, wrapped her arms around his neck and brushed her cheeks against his mustache. She took the lead and kissed him.

He whispered against her ear when she let him draw a breath. "There's cake at the reception that I need to get to. My family's waiting, and I want them all to meet you."

She covered his mouth with hers.

"Ummm." He pressed her back just a bit. "How is it that Kitty Franklin doesn't have anything to say?"

She inhaled. She didn't have anything to say to him, but between kisses she'd selected a few choice words for her father.

The office door creaked.

"Cousin Kitty? Uhh, that's you? I see now."

Kitty looked up. Davis tightened his hold. "What do you need, Glynnis?" Davis asked his new chief of staff.

Glynnis took a few steps closer, her eyes glued on the couple. "Mr. Thornton, the reporter and photographer from the Herald is here."

Davis gave Kitty a little nudge. "Give us five minutes, then send them in."

Glynnis tossed her blonde wig, her eyes still wide with surprise. "Sure. Cousin Kitty, I've been all over this place trying to find you. Your father wants you. Last place I would have thought to look."

"Okay, Glynnis, that's fine. I'm sure I know where to find him." Kitty stood. Before she stepped away, Davis caught her arm.

"Stay. I'm sure your father can wait a minute more. This should be a short interview: local boy comes home." He stood and stretched. "Maybe you can give me some advice or pointers. I like the way you handled that reporter earlier."

She shook her head. "No, it's the same one, and he doesn't need to see me in here with you. Like this." She straightened her skirt.

Davis looked down at her. "Lady, I'm not interested in being your closet boo."

She beamed. "It's not like that. Trust me, I know this guy and it's best not to give him any more material. Let me go see what the congressman wants. And give him a piece of my mind. Then I'm all yours."

"Uh, Miss Franklin, how do you propose getting out of here without running into said reporter?"

She walked towards a side door in the office. "It's not for nothing that Daddy and Bill Clinton are good friends. There's a passage through the butler's pantry."

Chapter 7

Hours later Kitty stood in what must have been Davis's childhood bedroom. Faded wallpaper of football scenes and local high school football pennants hung on the wall. A small dowel table covered with a lacy cloth holding a stack of Bibles stood next to the window. Across the room a tired-looking twin bed sat covered with a tattered college blanket. She was supposed to be out there meeting the Thornton family. A noisy host of cousins, family, and friends had assembled to welcome Davis home. Instead, she'd spent the past two hours in here working the phones.

Her father had given her the upside of this latest issue before he left the center. She could hardly believe her ears. This one was worse than the McNair affair. He didn't even apologize for ruining her weekend, just told her to contain it. She should have taken the time to properly meet Davis's mother before she answered the first call from the Washington press secretary. A new scandal was unfolding quickly. She stared at the e-copy of a court-ordered paternity test.

She plopped down on the twin bed and sank into the mattress. "How am I going to keep this from becoming a seven day sensation? It's one mess after another," she confided to Twanna during their third call in an hour. "I'm sorry, girl, but I'm going to need you to work through the weekend. Go to Daddy's office and watch them all. No interviews, no statements, and make it clear that no congressional staff hall chatting will go unnoticed." She clicked to answer her second line without saying goodbye.

"Yes?"

"Kitty, the press has surrounded the house." Her mother sounded calm, almost matter of fact.

She marched over to the window and drew the blinds shut. When was her father going to learn that his dark deeds always found light?

"Then stay inside and don't answer the door," she snapped. "Where's Daddy?"

"He went to play golf with the judge. They won't bother him there. Don't worry about us; we're not going out any more today. And Kitty, don't bother calling your father, he's not answering."

She clicked off her phone and took a deep breath. *He's not answering you, but I have a ringtone that always gets his response.* Her phone shook in her palm. She jumped. In rapid succession she fielded increasingly intense phone calls. Her head drooped as she tried to fight off the coming quake. She pulled at the chord of the cheap plastic blinds to try to block out the remaining sunshine that illuminated the Bibles on the table and the happy loudness of the Thornton family.

Davis leaned on the railing of his mother's front porch, nodding in time to his uncle's banter.

"I say ain't no Kitty Franklin in there," Ralph Branch, his maternal uncle scoffed.

"Yeah is," Charlie, his father's youngest brother, whistled from his perch on the swing. "Met her myself before her phone went berserk and she went in that there back room." Charlie wheezed and shook his wrinkled finger at Davis. "Boy, that's danger there," he coughed. "Messsin' with the farmer's daughter."

Ralph walked over to sit with Charlie. "Sho right."

Davis smiled at his uncles. In-laws for years, now through marriage and loss they were as close as any brothers. The stalwarts of the deacon board sat together and rocked.

"But I see what you see. She's a pretty little piece, looks just like her mama. That Yesenia Franklin is a well-preserved woman." Charlie ended with a fit of coughing.

Louvenia Thornton stepped onto the porch with a pitcher of water and three tall glasses. "Stop teasing Davis."

"Uh-huh. Lou, now you need to go on back in the house." Her brother Ralph stood to take the tray she carried. "We's talking men talk. We just trying to tell this boy right, with his father gone and all. And all I'm sayin' is that I know Roosevelt Franklin and I don't think it wise for our Dave here to be messing 'round with his daughter."

Charlie raised his hand to speak but the coughing cut him off. They waited for him to recover. "Thanks for the water, Lou." Charlie wheezed a quick breath. "Ralph right. The way folk been used and abused up at that center. Hired today…" Charlie hacked.

"If you know Roosevelt Franklin." Ralph finished.

"And fired tomorrow if Yesenia doesn't like it," Charlie spit out.

Ralph hooted. "Mark my word, Davis, see what happen if you make that little ole gal cry."

"Go", hack, hack, "running back to Daddy," Charlie spit out and bent over. Ralph poured out a glass of water and held it out for Charlie.

"Sorry, fellas, that 'physema get to going." His voice raspy from the strain of the cough, Charlie sat back, weakened. He took of sip from the glass Ralph offered.

"Should have quit smoking when I did, big fella." Underneath Ralph's dig, the concern in his eyes spoke volumes of the love and respect he held for his brother-in-law.

Davis stretched. "Thanks, Unks. I'll go see if Kitty's finished. I want you to meet her."

He stopped at the door to look back at his elderly uncles. They sat in silence, enjoying the time they had remaining with each other. He knocked three times on the solid pine door frame. It was so good to be home. The tiny ranch house his parents bought when he was in grade school had cleared out some. Most of the family had congratulated, eaten, and gone on about their business.

"That little woman's got a wicked whip for a tongue," his mother yelled as he passed the opening for the kitchen.

He heard Kitty's voice from his room across the hall, chewing somebody out in large lawyer words. A surge of excitement coursed through his body. She was one powerful little woman. He opened the door to his childhood bedroom. Something was wrong. The blinds were drawn and Kitty paced the floor slowly, like a big cat stalking prey. Her mouth, however, ran fast like a cheetah. She spoke almost a hundred words per minute. He couldn't quite see in the dim, but her eyes appeared to be closed. And just like a hunting cat she sensed his presence and moved closer. With a slow, deliberate movement she clicked her BlackBerry to mute.

She stretched on her toes in her pumps and kissed his cheek. "I'm sorry. I'm done here in a minute."

The other party yelled through her earpiece. He looked down at her face. Her eyes were closed. A vein throbbed prominently at her left temple. There was just enough light filtering through the shade for him to see the prescription bottle on the table, alongside his mother's Bibles.

"This is the last call? I'll go get some water for those pills."

She nodded and un-clicked the mute button. "Now that you've spoken your piece, do exactly what I said. Let's try to keep the national lid on this thing until Monday. Maybe by then something of real significance will have happened and this will die."

Davis backed out of the room and shut the door behind him. His mother stood in the doorway of her bedroom just a few steps away.

"Am I going to have to burn some incense and have the pastor come out and re-sanctify my prayer room?"

Davis's hearty laughter filled the small hall.

"Dave, I'm going to change my clothes. The only reason I kept this suit on for so long is because we had company, but I guess she done made herself at home." Louvenia shut her door. Davis stepped across the hall into the kitchen.

When he reopened the door of his bedroom it was just in time to race across the room and catch Kitty in mid-fall. He held her in one arm and placed the now half-filled glass of water on the table. "What happened?"

She spoke slowly. "It all went dark."

"Should I call a doctor?"

"No, this has happened before. I'm all right." She reached around Davis's bent frame, her hand in search of her BlackBerry. Quicker and with a longer wingspan, he plucked the device from the floor. She attempted to snatch it from his hand.

"No, enough of this," he whispered and held her phone high. "Come on." He helped her into a straight-back chair.

Kitty leaned back in the chair, then surged forward. He caught her, steadied her, and moved into action. "I'm going to forward these calls to Twanna. Then I'm going to call your parents and let them know what's going on and that I'll take care of you. Then I'm turning this thing off."

Howls of hello and laughter shot through the small house. A second round of friends and family must have entered.

She reached up to hold her head. "Shhh. How many people are in this little house? A hundred?" she hissed.

Davis glanced up. "We're loud people when we're happy. We're just glad to be together today, and I really want all of them to meet you. But you need to lie down." He slipped her BlackBerry into the pocket of his trousers and picked up the prescription bottle. "How many of these do you need to take?"

"Four."

He shook his head and read the label. "I'm not going to let you do this to yourself. It says here one to two pills every four hours as needed." He held her hand and dispensed two light blue oblong tablets into her palm.

Her lips pursed, the way they did before she verbally pounced. Her face and body contracted. She swallowed the pills and slumped.

She gave no protest when he scooped her up and carried her rigid body to the rickety twin bed he'd uncomfortably slept in for the past week. Why hadn't his mother purchased a new bed for this room? He wanted to lie down with her, but not here.

Davis turned and walked out of his room to his mother's. He gently laid Kitty on his mother's new bed. He stood for a moment and stared at the suffering woman. She covered her eyes with her hand. He longed to lie down beside her and massage the tension from her neck and body. How had he come to feel so deeply for this woman? Over two short weeks they had shared some of the most intimate details of their lives through phone conversations, e-mails, and text messages. He believed they'd formed a real bond. But being with her today had revealed their relationship had some real issues.

He hated duplicity, and the way he was forced to conceal his hiring from her still bothered him. Before the press conference, he'd stood up to her father and man-to-man let him know in no uncertain terms that going forward, his relationship with Kitty was not up for manipulation. The congressman said he'd earned his respect for speaking up.

"Can I get you anything else?"

"Something to block out the light." The last vestiges of the Carolina sunshine illuminated the corners of the room.

"I'll get you a cold compress."

"I don't want anything wet," she whipped out.

"Okay, Kitty." His shoulders slumped just a bit as he went to the master bath to fetch Miss Kitty a face cloth. Would he ever get used to her rudeness? He'd dated a woman for a year before she grew mean enough to tell him she stayed with him because he was everything she wanted, except for being too fat. When he broke up with her, he'd promised himself that he'd never accept that kind of meanness from a woman again.

And what's the difference between rude and mean?

He returned with a fresh face cloth for her to lay across her eyes.

"Davis, I can't. I need to..." Her voice was almost inaudible. The pain was still visible in the blue line that throbbed at her temple.

"You just need to lie down here and relax."

"Thank you, Action."

He smiled and left her to the quiet of his mother's room.

Kitty opened her eyes and looked around. A profusion of yellow flowers greeted her. Too many small yellow flowers, everywhere. From the bedspread to the quilted wall hangings. There was even a vase of silk happiness on the dresser. Ick. She sat up, closed her eyes, and listened. The house was quiet. She turned and read the alarm clock. It was already after eight. And beside the clock on a nightstand covered with a big yellow doily was her BlackBerry.

She smiled and swung her legs over to sit on the edge of the bed. She hesitated before hitting the on button. Afraid Davis might hear and come in before she could check on her father's situation, she slipped the phone under a yellow throw pillow as it went through its start-up. Sixty-two voice and text messages, mainly from media outlets. The story had broken. Twanna had sent the video clip of the piece that would run on CNN for the next twelve hours. She didn't bother to watch it, since she knew all the sordid details. Or at least the ninety percent her father had shared with her this afternoon. There was always the ten percent more that he'd held back. But this time she knew what that was, too. She scrolled through her messages and only read one.

I GOT THIS. LET BIG FINE TAKE CARE OF YOU. LYLAS T.

She replied to Twanna that she loved her like a sister, too. Kitty paused for a minute before she stood. She slipped on her four-inch heels and ventured slowly from the yellow room, following Davis's rich, melodic voice.

Davis, his sister Sharon, and their mother sat around a small table in the kitchen. It was a little yellow in there, too.

Davis stood to meet her. "Hey, honey? How do you feel? Are you hungry?"

His mother stood and went to fussing with pots on the stove.

"Mom, will you heat up a plate?" he asked.

Kitty shrugged. "Where's my purse? I need to fix my face."

Davis put an arm around her shoulder. "You don't have to do that for my family. Most of them are gone."

"I want to do it for you."

He grinned and walked her over to the table and pulled out the fourth chair. "You look fine, Kitty. Come sit down."

Sharon twisted in her seat. "What do you think about Mother's new room? We just redecorated it."

Davis held his breath.

Kitty knew him well enough to know if she insulted his mother it would be an unpardonable sin. "The jessamine is a lovely flower. The only thing missing from the room was the flower's wonderful fragrance."

Sharon seemed satisfied. Lou clanged the pots.

A melamine dinner plate landed in front of her. Macaroni with a thick slab of cheese oozed orange oil and a healthy portion of fat meat accented the collard greens. His mother obviously still cooked with ham hocks. There was a hunk of fresh honey-glazed South Carolina smoked ham and a homemade yeast roll glistening with butter. The aroma of pork and butter swept up her nose. Yuck. Yuck spewed all over the table. Davis jumped up as she pushed back. Yuck all over the floor.

Lou yelled above the screech of the skidding chairs, "If you have any more, try to make it to the sink."

Kitty heaved and shuffled to the sink and saw the remains of the meal dried on dozens of plates and pots. Spent glasses half full of amber liquid lined the counter and one glass appeared to be filled with phlegm. Yuck.

"It's too hot in here for her. Davis, take her out on the porch," Sharon said.

"That girl better not be pregnant, Dave," Lou yelled from her perch by the stove.

Davis led her out of the back door onto the large deck that ran the length of the house. Kitty relied on his strength and kept her eyes closed. Pine and roses scented the air. A light clicked on and she burrowed into his sleeve like a small woodland animal. "The light sensitivity is setting in. I need my sunglasses."

She pushed back from his arm when his pocket vibrated. He answered.

"It's your father. Are you okay to talk to him?"

"Give it to me."

"Wait a minute." He spoke to them both. Davis helped her settle in a porch chair before he handed her his phone. "I'll ask Mom to turn the porch light off."

Kitty listened as her father expressed his displeasure over her inability to control the press. When he finished she spoke slowly, afraid the intensity of yelling would bring a second blow from her headache. "Just one thing, Daddy," she hissed. "I'll take care of this, like I always do. But if you ever threaten Davis again, I'm through. And I'll go to the press myself and you know what I know. Bye."

She clicked off the phone and opened her eyes. The expanse of their backyard lay before her. In the distance a light shined above the door of a tool shed. The porch door slapped and Sharon stood wide-eyed at the door. A tray with crackers and a glass of 7-Up wobbled in her hand.

"Wow. I can't believe you talk to the congressman, your father, like that." Sharon walked over and offered her the glass.

Kitty rubbed her temple. Her eyes focused on the tool shed that Mr. Thornton had most likely used to store his tools and work on real projects. Unlike her father's high-tech spy shed. She took a deep breath and closed her eyes. "I'm sure your father never did the things my daddy does. But, I'm sorry you heard that." Kitty planted her feet on the wood plank porch and stood. "I think I'd better go back in there and apologize to your mother and leave before I get sick again."

Sharon shifted her footing. "Wait, sit back down for a minute before you go in." Sharon sat down beside her. "My brother's a really a nice man, and he hasn't dated a lot." She paused. "He's a grown man now, but I still think of him as my little brother. And people haven't always been nice to him because of his weight. I hope you're not playing with him. I don't want to see him abused."

Kitty's face twitched. "Your brother's beyond nice. He's wonderful and…" She stood and used the porch rail to steady herself. "Davis probably told you that I tend to speak my mind."

"He warned us."

"Sharon, do you think it's too soon for me to say I love your brother?"

Chapter 8

Waking up in a strange room was becoming a staple of her relationship with Davis. Kitty rolled over and hugged a pillow as a wave of security washed over her. She was safe in Davis's house, in his bed. She slipped out of bed and wandered through the house in search of her special agent.

Davis looked up from placing books in a newly built bookcase. "Feeling better?" Tools and cardboard boxes scattered his home construction site.

Kitty inched into the room. No furniture, so she tested a sturdy-looking box and sat. Davis started collecting his tools. "Kitty, what happened? I mean, you were fine when you left my office, before you met with your father. Does this headache have something to do with him?"

What her father told her today had shattered the last bit of faith she had in him. Kitty's eyes traced a dark line in the rug from one end to another. She shouldn't tell him any of this. He wasn't a member of the family. If he's turned on the TV, he already knows.

"I hope you feel you can trust me."

Her heart surged in her chest. She needed someone she could trust. "My father…" She paused. "It seems my father…" She stopped. Her head hung low. "My father has a son."

Davis gasped. "So the rumors about Linda McNair are true?"

"Yes and no. This boy's seventeen."

The wrench in his hand hit the floor with a thud.

"I shouldn't have to tell you this. It's on CNN," she snapped as fresh tears rained down her cheeks. "But I just can't believe it. And what he's asked me to do, to get involved in this." She sobbed, the tears coming faster. "To represent him in this matter." She sniffed and sighed. "I was always Daddy's special girl. Even after Dena was born he said that I would always be his special one. He called me his son. And for seventeen years he's known there was this boy growing up just miles from us in Anacostia."

Davis moved towards her box. He pulled her onto the floor and he held her close until the worst was over.

She sniffled. "His media consultant wants him to make a public statement. You know, one of those sorry affairs when the poor wife stands by her man and looks shell shocked. I worked all afternoon to kill that idea. Next week I'm going to fire his media consultant." Fearfully, she looked into his eyes and read compassion and kindness instead of disdain. "But that's not all," she sighed. "He wants me to sit with him next week when he meets with the mother. Daddy wants me to negotiate a new financial settlement. Apparently he's always supported this child. I just never knew."

Davis's head snapped back as he remembered Roosevelt's comment about a man always providing. "Does your mother know?"

Her eyes rolled up to the ceiling. "Probably. No one knows what goes on with those two. Or why I spent our afternoon bothering to protect her. If Daddy asked, she'd play the good wife and stand by his side as she's done so many times before." She slumped a little in his arms.

Davis squeezed a little tighter. "You did the right thing, and, honey, I'm sure this has nothing to do with how your father feels about you. What I'm wondering is why now, if he's been paying all along?"

"Now? Now the boy's preparing for college. He's going to Georgetown, like Dena. The mother not only wants Daddy to pay for it, she wants him to spend more time with her son. To publicly acknowledge him in an election year."

"What does your father say?"

She wiggled away from him and stood. "He says she's a single mother with a middle-class income. He wants her to file for federal financial aid. He says he's willing to take care of the rest financially on the side, but she isn't going for it. She wants public recognition and the Georgetown tuition."

Davis stood and wrapped his arms around her from behind. "Kitty, you keep saying she. Do you know this woman?"

She sat back down. He joined her and she snuggled in close to him. "Toni was his chief of staff fifteen years ago when I first worked in Daddy's office. She befriended me; she was like a mentor. She showed me all the ins and outs and hidden passages of the Capitol. I even babysat for her son once," she sobbed.

Davis turned her around and kissed her swollen eyelids. That blue vein slowly throbbed at her temple. She reached up and tried to wrap her arms around his neck. "Come down here and kiss me."

Between his kisses she murmured, "Take me to bed."

His body responded immediately, and his hardened penis pressed against her thigh.

"Oh, baby, I don't know." He kissed her neck. "I don't want to take advantage."

"Take me to bed," she pleaded. "I don't want to ruin our weekend."

His face constricted and his mustache quivered. The rough softness of his facial hair scratching her neck caused her knees to shake. Davis picked her up and carried her to the bedroom.

Within minutes he was deep inside her. His manhood was larger than she'd suspected. In the midst of his thrust she blurted, "When you come I'm going to spit out semen."

His hands encircled her waist and rolled them over. Then he lifted himself from her. "I'm hurting you?"

My damn mouth. "No, baby, it feels good." She urged him back on top of her. He settled and rocked back and forth. She bent forward to try and meet his lips. Davis thrust into her depths.

"Ugh, oh, oh baby, yes," she cried. *Come, please come. Oh, this is killing me.* "Oh, God, yes."

Davis rolled over and panted.

Her stomach contracted and she took in a breath. The air burned her lungs. In the dark his erection stood like an obelisk between them. She drew another breath and closed her eyes tightly. She wanted so badly for this unconventional relationship to work and good, satisfying sex would be an important part. She drew in another breath and disregarded her aching thighs. She wanted to satisfy him more than anything. She climbed atop him and inched herself lower toward his shaft. She pushed her breast against his penis and began a slow undulation. Up and down. Up and down.

Davis groaned.

She rocked and used her arms to keep her breast close. He began to thrust. She lowered her head and flicked the tip of his penis with her tongue. They moved in unison. He up, she down. Her heart sang. She inched closer and took his head into her mouth. He filled her mouth but didn't thrust. She moved forward taking him in.

Davis groaned while she suckled. "Oh, girl."

Davis reached climax and lifted her up toward his face. "That's good," he blew out.

"I love you."

"Me, too, baby." He gave her a quick kiss on the right shoulder and rolled out of bed.

Where you going? lay at the tip of her tongue. She bit her lip and swallowed to hold the comment in. *If you want to be with him you are going to have to keep your mouth shut. You'll get used to him, all of him.*

"Here, baby." He held out a warm wash cloth.

"Thank you. You're so sweet." *Thank God, because I don't think I can walk.*

He crawled back into bed and pulled her close.

"Davis?" she whispered.

"Hummm?" His voice was heavy with sleep.

"Davis, we should talk."

He kissed her shoulder. "Aw, girl, you laid me out. All I want to do right now is sleep."

"I want things to be good between us. Everything, Davis."

He yawned. "Me, too."

"Next time I'll…"

"I'm satisfied. Unless you want to do what you just did again." He pulled her body closer to his and murmured, "It's been a long day. Let's get some rest."

Kitty yawned and stretched. She rolled over. After a good night's sleep she sat up lazily in bed. She ran her hand across the sheets. He'd been up for so long the sheets were cold. She glanced around the room at the boxes and furniture that still needed to be set up, details she'd missed last night. She stretched again. Voices. Davis and a woman? The smell of coffee, bacon, and fresh bread filled the room.

"It's either his mother or sister. I'd better get up."

She took a nice long shower and dressed in an aqua silk sweater, blue jeans, and high-heeled boots. She listened as she walked towards the kitchen. It's his mother.

"Good morning."

"Day's half gone," Lou replied.

She looked around for a clock. Maybe she had slept too long. On her way to the kitchen she'd noticed that Davis had advanced the work she'd interrupted last night in the den. His home office was almost set up.

"Morning, babe. It's only ten o'clock." Davis stood by the stove looking fine. He wore a pair of baggy shorts over the spandex running tights Twanna had been talking about for the past two weeks.

Lou eyed Kitty. "Like I was saying, I've already been to the farmers' market and the grocery store."

"You must have gotten up early to get all that accomplished."

Lou crossed her arms over her chest. "No, actually I slept late. Didn't get up till six."

Kitty smiled politely and walked over to sit down in the bay window seat. She'd have to let his mother get away with her comments. She smirked at the purple and olive grapevine pattern that covered the cushion and the ugly matching valence. She looked at Davis's mom sitting at the small table covered with a white plastic tablecloth and the soda bottle full of yellow and white flowers, fresh from the market.

"Dave called and said he didn't have a table in here so his princess would have a proper place to sit and eat breakfast, so I had to go out to the shed and find this old card table and chairs, clean them up, and get them over here in time. Made me late for the farmers' market. By the time I got there the fruit was picked over, but I did get some good greens for tomorrow," Lou fussed. "But it seems I got here in time. Dave wanted me to mix up some biscuits for breakfast."

"I'll just have some coffee."

"Girl, you better eat my momma's biscuits," Davis chimed in. "Now how do you want your eggs?"

"Ain't but one way to have eggs." Lou stood up. "Dave, what are you doing?"

His mother nudged him aside. "Those eggs came from the farmers' market. You need to crack each one in a separate bowl."

"Why?" Kitty asked as she moved to sit at the table.

"Because if one of them's been fertilized…" Lou began.

"How would you know?"

"Lord, what do they teach in law school?" Lou clucked. "If it has a red dot, that's means it's been fertilized. And if it mixes in with the other eggs, we'll throw them all out."

Kitty looked at Davis and then his mother.

"We respect the potential for life, all life," Lou said.

Kitty's mind raced back several years to when her politically correct father had come into their mother's parlor and set aside all of his public statements to issue a simple plea to her older sister: "Don't kill my grandbaby," he'd said.

"You look so far away. What you thinking about, Princess?" Lou asked.

She jumped. "My niece, Quanny."

"That's right, I almost forgot Congressman Franklin had a grandbaby." Lou nodded and sat down at the table. "The problem ain't the babies, it's the sin that goes before them."

Lou was more astute than she'd first thought. In two concise statements Lou had given Kitty her view of abortion and called her a sinner.

Davis came to the table with two plates overflowing with steaming eggs, biscuits, and bacon. He set a plate down in front of his mother, then served Kitty.

"Can I get you ladies anything else?"

"Yes, you forgot the grits." Lou raised her fork at Kitty. "You do eat grits?"

Kitty smiled. "Yes, with lots of butter."

"Me, too." Lou smiled. "Davis, bring our grits in bowls if you have some clean. I don't know how you invite anyone to stay in a half unpacked house. You need anything else, Princess?"

She shifted in her chair. "Do you have any honey for the biscuits?"

Lou raised her hands and clapped. "You do know how to eat. Dave, bring the honey. It's in one of those bags from the farmers' market. That's one of the reasons I stopped by the market early. Our friend's a beekeeper, and I wanted to get you a jar of his spring honey. If you like it, take it back to Washington with you."

Kitty smiled at Lou's kind gesture and backhanded slap. Davis served the grits and set out the honey.

"Aren't you going to join us?" Kitty asked.

"Oh, no. I've got things to do at the stove."

Lou picked up her fork and began an interrogation. She asked about everything a mother would want to know. Lou was as thorough in her questioning as any opposing counsel Kitty had ever faced. Kitty obliged and kept her answers succinct and respectful. Davis was worth it. Thankfully, the interview didn't last long before Davis announced that they had somewhere to go.

"Okay, you two go ahead. I'll stay and clean the kitchen. Sharon and I have an appointment at the beauty shop today at two to get our hair done for tonight. She wanted me to invite you to come with us."

Kitty ran a hand across her bob. She had just had it washed and styled before she left DC.

"That's a good idea," Davis answered for her. "That'll work. I'll bring her by before I go to get my haircut."

Before she could protest Davis took her hand and hurried her out the door. As they drove away she commented on his mother's questioning techniques. "Boy, your mother is nosy."

"Why didn't you tell her to stop?"

"When was the last time you were able to stop your mother when she was trying to prove a point?"

He laughed.

"By the way, she's not happy with my staying with you." She shrugged. "And neither are my folks. My grandmother in particular."

Chapter 9

Davis drove them out to Kings Mountain State Park.

He walked with her up to what looked like a mini-Washington Monument. "I know you need to think about what's happened with your father. It's not the Washington Monument, but maybe it'll help. I'm going to run." He jogged in place to warm up. "I'll leave you to your thoughts."

She watched his powerful legs as he jogged away from her. Her heart warmed because he'd remembered. "Davis?" she called after him.

He didn't look back.

She moved closer to read the inscription on the obelisk. It was dated 1815, making it the second oldest Revolutionary War monument in the nation. Impressive, but not impressive enough to convince her that her world hadn't come to an end.

She'd always been Daddy's special girl. At five her favorite game was playing congresswoman in his study. She was the one he took on the campaign trail and lobbyist junkets. Daddy and Kitten were always on the same team for family game night. She walked around the obelisk, a short trip.

"How could he do this to me?"

Wasn't it bad enough that she'd spent most of her childhood sleeping in an adjourning hotel room while he had sex with staffers, political junkies, and campaign volunteers? She swiped her tears with the sleeve of her sweater. She should have said something to her mother, especially that first summer she worked in the office, when she figured out what was going on. Her father had spent too much time behind locked doors with his chief of staff, Toni. But that summer he'd also spent a lot of time with her, taking her to lunch in the congressional dining room and allowing her to serve as his page on the floor of the house. That summer he'd encouraged her interest in the law and politics. He'd known what he was doing when he made her his personal attorney. He'd trained her to be a loyal, silent accomplice. Her own father had manipulated and trapped her.

She loved him dearly, but this was too much. He'd actually asked her to negotiate a financial settlement with Toni Jacobs, her former mentor and his son's mother. And she'd have to do her best because if she failed him, nothing would outweigh her guilt.

Tears spilled over. She rested on a green recycled wood bench and tried to force back the tears. She stood up and made another trip around the monument.

She was going to have to draw a line. She could no longer be her father's son, and it was going to hurt her far more than it would him. She inhaled some fresh South Carolina air and thought of Davis. Good and perfect so far, Davis.

She pulled her BlackBerry from her jacket and read only the latest text from Twanna.

WAS IT AS BIG AS IT LOOKS?

She grinned and keyed in a reply. OMG UR FOUL.

Then she turned it off and decided not to turn it on, read any papers, or watch any news until Tuesday. "I don't care what happens. For the next two days I'm going to focus on you." She pointed towards the man that lumbered toward her. "Yea, Davis." She clapped and cheered as he jogged toward her. Big, fine, sexy, kind, sweaty Davis. She stepped up on the park bench. "Yea, Dave."

He jogged up to her and she wrapped her arms around his neck.

"Hey, I'm taller than you." She bent her neck to kiss him.

He pulled back slightly. "Wait, baby, I think I might smell a little strong."

Kitty interlocked her fingers behind his neck. "Smells sexy. Now why don't you take off those baggy shorts and show me those jogging pants Twanna's still talking about?"

A sheepish grin covered his face. "Shorts stay on." He peeled her arms from his neck so he could stretch. He plopped his foot up on the bench and stretched his powerful hamstring. "Do you think she talks too much?"

Kitty reached over and tugged at his shorts. "Yes, that's why I don't tell her anything."

A smirk of disbelief covered his face as he switched legs.

"Well, nothing personal." She kissed his glistening forehead.

He finished his after-run routine with a gulp of water. "It's time for me to give you up. I'll drop you at the beauty shop before I clean up."

She hopped down from the bench to follow him to the car. "I hadn't planned to have my hair done."

"Shorty, you know this isn't about getting your hair washed."

"That's why I don't want to go."

He held the car door open for her. "It's up to you. But can I ask why you have the same haircut as your mother? You know, it kind of freaks me out that you two look so much alike."

A few hours later Kitty swayed under a sweltering heat. She was trapped by a too-hot hair dryer in a beauty shop in a bonding ritual with Davis's mother and sister. Why'd she let the stylist talk her into trying a new hairstyle? She watched the screen door of the shop close behind Davis for a second time. He'd come to pick her up. But since her hair wasn't dry, he'd gone next door to a sweets shop and brought her a snack. Sweet iced tea and a bag of chips. They sure did a lot of eating. No wonder he used to be fat.

She leaned forward under the hood and tried to make out what the women were saying through the humming hot dryer. From the hoots and catcalls and high fives, she knew it was some good bad girl talk. And she sensed it was about Davis. She lifted the dryer's bonnet.

The shampoo assistant was just finishing her assessment. "That man wasn't that fine when he left here."

"Ummm-ummm. I'd let that man wear me out all night, evr'y night and then get up and cook him breakfast in the morning," the client in the shop owner's chair threw out.

"There a BMW, with a paid-for BMW in the neighborhood." A tall attractive young woman with a shower cap covering a freshly washed Beyoncé weave reached for the cell phone she had holstered at her hip. "Let me call my pastor to get the church ready." The shop erupted in laughter.

Kitty hopped up. "Wait, ladies. That's my man," she hollered over the din.

Leticia, the shop owner, picked up a small barrel marcel curling iron from her station's stove and twirled it around in the air to cool. "Oh, no, she didn't come out from under that dryer."

"Yes, she did. Claim your man, Kitty." Davis's sister lifted her hand and stepped over to Kitty with her hand held high for five.

"Now what's a petite, proper, no-booty little Eastern girl with something white in her hair that's not gonna draw up a good knot at the end of the night, gonna know what to do with a man like that?" Leticia twirled the iron again and stepped around her chair in front of her client. When she had the floor Leticia swung her ample hips out. "It takes a good thick-hipped-nappy-headed southern gal to take care a' all that."

The patrons all shouted. Leticia looked behind her. Lou was being curled at the next station. "Uh, sorry, Lou, no disrespect."

Lou threw up her hand and shook her head. Laugher constricted her voice.

Kitty took two more steps towards Leticia and entered the center ring of the shop to square off with the owner. "Let me get you all straight right now. I know exactly what to do with my BMW and ladies," she swished her hips out from side to side, "what I do, he likes." She lifted her arm up, snapped her fingers in the air and stepped back to her dryer. The shop erupted in hoots and howls.

The client in Leticia's chair spoke out again. "Lady, you need to get back over here, put that iron back in the fire, and curl up my head. 'Cause the lawyer done made her case."

Kitty looked around the shop. Her eyes landed on Lou. She winced. "I'm sorry, I didn't mean to disrespect you, Mrs. Thornton."

Lou's lips turned into an upside-down smile. "Have mercy."

Kitty pulled the dryer bonnet back down on her hair. She'd gained some ground in the shop; the conversation should shift to another topic. She twisted the dryer's setting to cool and picked up last month's Essence. Behind the pages of the magazine her face erupted into a full grin. She was talking jive with the home folks, as Daddy called it. She bit the inside of her jaw.

Davis did look good when he came in. His jeans fit his booty nicely; he'd just had a shave, shower, and haircut. The man was looking and smelling just right. The barber's aftershave had a nice citrus spice. She wasn't a religious woman, but she thanked the Lord he was her man. She glanced at her watch and hoped her hair would hurry and dry. Davis was coming back in an hour.

Thirty minutes later Leticia stood over her and chastised, "Girl, why'd you turn that dryer down?" She pulled out one of the straws in Kitty's hair.

"It ain't set right." Leticia spritzed her again with setting lotion. Down south hair had to be hard dried with lots of product.

"You have to turn the dryer past fifteen for it to properly heat up," she said as she backed Kitty under the bonnet.

She wasn't ready when Davis returned, so he took his mother home and Sharon waited with her.

∽✧∾

"Do I look all right?" Kitty asked shortly after 6 p.m. as they sped toward the Center.

Davis stared straight ahead and tightened his grip on the steering wheel. "Fine."

"Do you like my hair?"

He leaned forward and focused on the road. "It's fine."

Sure now Davis was paying her no attention, she poked her lip out and stared out the window. "Did you even notice the color of my dress?" She smoothed the skirt of her strapless green velvet evening gown. The matching caplet that she would put on once they reached the Center almost slipped to the floor.

At the next light Davis bent forward and rested his head on the steering wheel.

"Kitty, I'm sure you look fine. I've got a few issues pressing on my mind right now. We had a problem in the kitchen earlier. I'm speaking in less than two hours and your father is not happy with me for leaving the Center to come pick you up before he introduced me to the mayor."

She reached over and placed a hand on his thigh. The light changed, and she held her tongue. After all, he was the motivational speaker and she was the girl who always said the wrong thing.

His hand nudged hers.

She turned her palm over and their fingers interlaced. She held on to his firm grasp. As they neared the Center his grip loosened. His tension became hers. She was now worried about the evening's success.

They walked hand-in-hand into the Center and stopped in his office. From his desk he picked up a small flower box.

"You look very pretty tonight. I didn't know what your dress looked like so the florist said a wrist corsage was safest." He opened the clear box and slid a spray of perfectly formed jessamine onto her wrist.

"Such a sweet Southern gesture. Thank you."

Davis grinned. "You know I'm a country boy. Are you ready to go in and face your father?" Concern clouded his features.

Kitty wrapped her arms around him. "No, you go ahead. I'll come in a minute."

He gave her a light peck on the cheek. "Then I'm off to check on the kitchen, again."

Kitty took a deep breath to fortify herself. As angry as she was with her father, she would hold her peace tonight for Davis. "Please let this evening go smoothly." She spoke to the God she didn't quite believe in.

Kitty crossed the hall alone and entered the multipurpose room of the Center. The room had been transformed in one short day. She blinked twice. There wasn't a ballroom in Washington that could rival the tasteful black and white décor of this room in Rock Hill, South Carolina tonight. The decorations were minimal. Interwoven panels of black and white silks covered the ceiling and draped behind the head table. Low table decorations with all white flowers in simple black squares adorned each table. Even the large Christmas tree in the corner was decorated in black and white. This could not be Glynnis's work. It was too classy.

"Hello." An elderly couple stood with her in awe at the doorway.

"I've never seen the room look like this," the woman said.

"We're the Rivers." The gentleman extended his hand.

Kitty reached out and paused. She was at a loss for how to introduce herself. As her father's daughter or Davis's girlfriend?

"Kitty Franklin, and I think this might be the new director's doing." She smiled at the couple and excused herself. After a quick scan of the ballroom she headed to the reception table for a cup of punch. Kitty purposely chose the spot at the far side of the room to steer clear of her father. But from the corner of her eye she watched him politicking and gladhanding, as if he hadn't a care in the world. Her mother stood dutifully by his side, as if she hadn't been betrayed again.

"Hey, babe." Davis, tall, strong and true, stood behind her. "Want something stronger from the bar?"

"No, thank you. I've learned not to mix alcohol with my prescription drugs."

Concern filled his eyes. "Feeling okay?"

"I'm fine. But I was getting a little perturbed at that beauty salon, so I took a little something, just in case."

He extended his arm. "That was probably a good call, because your father wants to see you."

As they moved toward her parents, Davis stopped to introduce her as his girlfriend to several couples. He sounded so proud to claim her. They waited a moment when they reached the congressman, since he was holding court with a city councilman. Kitty tapped her foot.

"Is it okay that I introduce you as my girlfriend?" Davis said.

She shrugged. "Girlfriend sounds like we're twelve."

"Since both of our parents are here tonight, out of respect I can't introduce you as my lover, and if I called you my lady friend that would sound like we're sixty." Davis stepped behind her and whispered in her ear. "Kitty, you my woman."

She turned around to tease him for sounding so country. But he'd stepped away. She watched his broad back as he bent to hug someone. When she faced forward again her mother stood in front of her.

"Kitty, darling, what have you done to your hair?"

"You don't like it?"

"Well, it looks...does Davis like it?"

Her eyes rolled up toward the ceiling. She hated it when her mother vacillated. "Tell me what you think, Mommy."

"Well, it looks kind of country."

She exhaled. "I think so, too. The beautician said it would loosen up. I think I might like it better in a few days. But it's so hard and stiff."

"Baked in dryer set. It'll fall." Yesenia Franklin reached out with her left hand and caught her husband's arm. "Excuse me, Rosey, Kitty's here."

Her father finished his conversation with the city councilman who Kitty remembered to be a distant cousin before he turned. A scowl furrowed his brow as he gave her the once-over.

"Kitten, I'm not thrilled about how you've taken care of matters for me."

She took a deep breath. When he talked about work she preferred him to call her Catherine. "I have Twanna setting up a meeting at the law office." She glanced over at her impervious-looking mother.

"I hope you didn't tell her anything. She talks too much."

She rubbed her temples. "Just enough for her to do her job."

"Good, good." Roosevelt looked past her and waved at someone across the room. She knew his signals. He was done with her.

"Kitty, make sure you and Davis make it over to speak to your grandmother before she leaves tonight." Her mother reached out to give Kitty one of her customary two handed hugs. "Enjoy the evening, dear."

Her father's lip curled. "Try not to distract Davis too much from his work."

Kitty pulled at the lapels of her green caplet and stepped away from her parents. Her father's curled lip took her back in time. She was thirteen when her breasts blossomed and overbloomed. She was riding in the backseat of his sedan when she overheard him command her mother to teach her how to dress without distracting.

Kitty was just like her mother except for two things. Her mother was perfectly petite, and she would never take the kind of stuff from a man that her mother did.

A warm arm circled her waist from behind. Prince Charming had come to claim her, right on time. "Finished?" he murmured in her ear. "Come on, I want to make sure you see all of this."

Chapter 10

Davis escorted her across the parquet dance floor set up for later toward the Christmas tree. From this panoramic view of the room, the reception seemed to be going exceedingly well, all around tinks of glasses and laughter.

On Davis's signal a trumpeter in full marching band regalia stepped to the center of the room and blew out a royal welcome. Kitty looked up at Davis.

"It's my high school marching band." He beamed as twenty or so high school musicians followed a high-stepping drum major to the center of the room. The crowd stepped aside as the group joined in with the trumpeter to play "Hark the Herald Angels Sing." Kitty's stomach fluttered as the ensemble high stepped in their black and white spats across the dance floor, their gold capes swaying from side to side as they marched into a four-by-four square unit. The drum major held his baton aloft and brought the group to a sharp halt. The room erupted in applause. Kitty looked up at Davis, who brimmed with pride.

"I played in that band not so long ago," he said.

"They're great."

The drum major executed a series of elaborate baton twirls that signaled the drum line to strike up a cadence. Glynnis skidded across the dance floor, looking almost elegant in a sleek black evening gown. She waved her hands at the crowd. "That means y'alls supposed to take your seats."

Kitty shook her head at her country cousin. "What's that on top of her head?" While her dress was simple, Glynnis had apparently paid a hairdresser to dye her weave snow white and heap it on top of her head in a Christmas tree-like formation topped with a silver star.

Davis looked down at her. "Did I tell you that you look wonderful tonight? After our parents leave, I hope you'll take that little cape thing back off. You have pretty shoulders." He extended his arm and escorted her to the head table.

Kitty exhaled. She worked hard on her shoulders to keep them unscarred by bra straps. She was elated that he'd noticed. She took his arm and put her father's disapproving glare behind her.

After the dais party was seated, the band played "Amazing Grace" and high stepped out of the ballroom. Davis took his place behind the microphone and gave some introductory remarks as master of ceremonies for the evening. He held the audience in the palm of his hand with his charm and melodic voice as he introduced the head table and his family.

She marveled at how masterfully he handled his duties. Smooth. Real smooth.

"Last, but certainly not least, my lovely date, Miss Catherine Franklin."

She gave the customary acknowledgement wave she'd learned from her mother.

"Dinner is served and for those of you who aren't sure that the musical blessing was sufficient, don't worry. I prayed with the kitchen and wait staff earlier. The food has been blessed. Please enjoy your dinner."

She was all smiles when he sat down beside her. During the meal he gave her his full attention. It was as if they were the only people in the room on this, the second of their unorthodox dinner dates. Comfortable under his attention, she wound her leg around his under the table.

"Kitty," he murmured in a low, sexy voice.

"I'm really hungry." She reached over for a forkful of green beans from his standard chicken dinner plate. "These are really good."

"That's some Southern seasoning. You want some more? I can ask them in the kitchen."

"No, I'll just eat yours."

"Kitty, Kitty," he purred.

She grinned as she chewed on her rubbery chicken. Just before dessert was served Davis excused himself to prepare for his speech. At the appropriate time Congressman Franklin stood at the podium to assume the host duties. As he made his usual remarks, Kitty played with the dry red velvet cake on her dessert plate and tried to tune him out. She'd heard his duplicity and lies many times before. She perked up when he began to introduce Davis.

"For some reason the women in my family meet Davis Thornton once and fall under some kind of spell. My wife, Yesenia, raved about him after he was the guest speaker at a church conference last year. Went on and on until I extended the invitation to him to speak here tonight. Again, I thank you, Mrs. Franklin, for your wisdom and foresight. Davis Thornton is an outstanding young man and I know we're going to be challenged and inspired by what he has to say. I'm just going to say this as I take my seat." Roosevelt motioned for Davis to join him. He shook Davis's hand and said to the crowd, "Stay away from my mother." The crowd erupted in howls of laughter as Franklin took his seat.

Kitty bit her lip. The Franklin women didn't need protection from Davis. She shifted in her chair as Davis took over the lectern. Within moments he had her and the entire room spellbound. His words were powerful. He spoke about change, which he called "shift." She thought about the shift she'd made yesterday, when she decided to tell Davis the intimate details about her father's son. Maybe she needed to make some more changes. Like growing up a little and moving outside of her father's influence. She'd thought about these things earlier today at the park, and, as Davis spoke, it all seemed so clear.

His voice rose to a crescendo. She shifted in her chair to give him her full attention.

"I've given this talk a few times before, but tonight the themes are so prominent in my own life that I'm speaking for myself as I work through some major shifts in my own life." He glanced down at her, winked, and continued. "You'd think moving home to the community I grew up in would be uneventful, but with this move so many new things have come."

Kitty swelled with pride as he brought his speech to a close. No wonder her mother had been so impressed by him. He was a great speaker. In one short twenty minute speech he'd motivated her to be his grown-up girlfriend. She sat up a little straighter and led the standing ovation when he finished.

Kitty shifted impatiently in her seat twenty minutes later as she waited for Davis to come back to the table. A minute ago she'd attempted to go to him. She knew he was in his office but her mother had stopped her. Yesenia said that in her experience it was best to let him come down off his speaker's high.

She shrugged off her annoyance with her mother. Yesenia patted her shoulder the way she had when Kitty was a child and said Davis would come back when he was ready. She glanced over at her mother sitting serenely next to her father as he glad-handed and guffawed.

Her mother certainly did know the role of first lady. She probably shouldn't be so hard on her. Maybe she could learn something from her about supporting a man. It was Yesenia's quiet dedication that had made the difference in the last election. All of the polling data spoke to how popular her mother was among the most steadfast voters in the black community, the church mothers. The women, who held the church together, managed the movement, and knew their history, always voted. And they voted conservatively, for the family values represented by Yesenia Franklin.

Several of the elders worked their way past the head table on their way out of the ballroom. Dinner and speeches finished, they were eager to get home before the dancing and in time to watch the ten o'clock news. She pasted on a smile. There was so much she wanted to say to Davis, but it would have to wait.

"Good night, Miss Franklin." An elderly gentleman extended his hand.

She rose and reached across the table and gave him a two-handed grip, just the way she'd seen her mother do for years. "Good night and thank you for coming."

"Make sure you tell that young man what a wonderful job he did. Masterful speech." The man's hand trembled as she released it.

"Yes, I will."

She held her position and received similar kind wishes from a number of other people. Her palm itched. She was already tired of playing this role. She wanted to congratulate Davis herself on his marvelous speech. She wanted to wrap him up in her arms and take him home. And she needed to speak with him in depth about shift, ask him how a person truly changed.

"Kitty? Davis said he'd be with you in just a minute," Glynnis whispered from behind her. "And cuz, you need to hold your hand over your chest when you lean over. You're giving the old men a show." Kitty turned around and scowled. It wasn't fair that Glynnis had got to him before she could. Her frown lightened when she noticed Mama Cat a few steps away, being wheeled over by Glynnis's date.

She bit her tongue. As much as she wanted to, she shouldn't comment now on Glynnis's hair, advice, or date. Her date was a twenty-something Hispanic-looking fellow with long super-straight hair pulled back into a ponytail for tonight's formal occasion.

"Kitty, that man." Her grandmother waved for emphasis. "Woo, I tell you what. You can let me know when and where he's speaking next. I won't miss it. That's a fine man both inside and out." Mama Cat actually had stars in her eyes.

"I guess Cousin Rosey's right. Davis got some magic with the Franklin women. Kitty-Kat, did you hear your gran say she might set foot in a BMA church just to hear Davis preach?" Glynnis said.

Kitty cringed. She hated being called Kitty-Kat, and Glynnis knew it. "Mama Cat's just talking."

"No, I'm not. That man's 'bout to make me go back on my word. I hear he can sing, to boot." The older woman fanned her face with her hand. "Woo." Mama Cat turned toward her reluctant escort. "I think I'll stay a while longer. Just leave me here to sit with my granddaughter."

Glynnis's lip twisted. "Mrs. Franklin, I think we should get you moving. The news will be on in a few."

"Now you wait just one minute." Mama Cat shooed Glynnis with her cane. "I want to stay a little longer, wait to see what else that Davis Thornton has to say."

Kitty grinned while Glynnis shifted from foot to foot. The only reason Mama Cat ever stayed out later than nine-thirty was if she had something she wanted to say. "I'm glad you like him so much. I do, too."

"Well, in my day we weren't so fast." Mama Cat pursed her lips. "But I'm not going to get started. You have your fun tonight and I'll talk at you later."

"Are you ready now?" The young man leaned in and leered at Kitty.

"Yeah, sure. Kitty, this is Rodrigo, Glynnis's date." She winked. "They're going to drive me home."

The whole time Rodrigo stood there he'd ogled Kitty's breasts. When addressed, he muttered hello to her bosom.

"Well, come on, Rod." Glynnis pushed him along. "Now be careful and pay attention to where you're going. If we hurry we'll be back before the party gets started good."

Kitty waved goodbye, then pulled her caplet closer. What a cougar!

Then there he was, standing behind her parents, no doubt accepting their congratulations for a job well done. Her father's hearty laugh irked her. Does he ever stop? She knew her father would hold him hostage for a few minutes so she pulled out her BlackBerry and sent Davis a text message.

LLTA, MEANING LOTS AND LOTS OF THUNDEROUS APPLAUSE.

Finally, he came to her. "Miss Kitty, are you ready to make our rounds?" He held the back of her chair.

She frowned at her handsome date. "Can't you sit a minute and talk?"

"I'm sorry, lady, but if I don't get over to that table and hear from my folks real soon, it's not going to be pretty."

She scanned the room and found the corner where the Thornton family sat. Stalwarts, their tables still full. Clearly no one was leaving until they spoke to the man of the hour.

She pasted on her mother's political wife smile. "Okay."

Chapter 11

"And this is…" She'd smiled and nodded through what seemed like endless introductions, all the school friends, church members, and family members she'd failed to meet yesterday.

"This is Uncle Charlie," Davis announced proudly.

At last, the last one. She'd never remember all their names. How could she? No wonder it had sounded like a fully loaded political rally in that little house yesterday. Davis had a huge family, and even more of them had come out tonight to support him. He'd firmly held onto her hand throughout the intros and polite questions. She squeezed his hand in thanks for his support.

"You sit yourself down here, Miss Lady." Uncle Charlie indicated an empty chair right between him and Uncle Ralph.

Davis dropped her hand. "I need to go check on a few things. Can I leave you here for a minute?"

Kitty sat in response.

Davis placed a hand on her shoulder and gave it a quick caress. "Uncle Ralph, now you watch my girl around this rascal." Davis pointed at his Uncle Charlie, chuckled, and strode away.

Kitty took a deep breath; this interview was probably just as important as her audience with Lou this morning. Davis had told her all about his family patriarchs. His family seemed so different from hers. Both sides of his family were traditionally led by solid, decent, faithful, family men who were nothing like her father.

"Well, Miss Kitty Franklin, I'm right glad we get a chance to talk to you," Charlie started.

She looked at the table. Everyone else had politely left. "I'm sorry we couldn't chat yesterday."

Charlie reached up, blotted his eyes and took a raspy breath. "You couldn't help it if you took sick."

Ralph nodded.

Charlie wiped his mouth with his handkerchief. "She's just as pretty as her mother. Ain't she, Brute?"

Ralph nodded again.

"Looked just like her yesterday but... What did you do to your hair?" Charlie asked.

She reached up and patted her tight curls. "Uh?"

Ralph moved his chair closer to the table. "Miss Kitty, did your mother ever tell you about your Uncle Charlie here?"

"Well, I'm sure she's mentioned him," she hedged to be polite.

Charlie waved his hand and coughed. "Now let me tell it." He gagged and turned his head as he was overcome with a series of coughs, spits, and gurgles.

Ralph shot her a look that implored patience.

Charlie looked as if he might be smaller than she was. The way his head poked out of his formal suit reminded her of a turtle with large, watery eyes. Davis had told her that his uncle had been an important man in the community before the ravages of emphysema reduced him to a shell of a man in an oversized suit.

Charlie pushed his soiled cloth deep into his pocket and pulled out another. "Well, I guess you better go head and tell it." His turtle-like head lowered into his jacket.

"What Charlie is trying to say is that Davis might a been yo cousin." Uncle Ralph winked at her.

"Now," hack hack, "you don't need to go dredging up old history." Charlie leaned over a bit.

Her eyebrows shot up. Her mother never spoke about any of her former relationships. Not doing so was a part of her mother's teachings. But through old gossip and her grandmother she had heard that there was someone in Rock Hill before her father. Could it be Charlie? She directed her gaze at Uncle Charlie. "Did you ever date my mother?"

"Hoo hoo," Ralph hooted. "No, that was somebody else. Charles was just a friend and classmate. He was one of the first people your mother met when she came here for college. They took their first college courses together. They were lab partners, but Charlie was studying Yesenia. He always said your mother was the prettiest student they ever had. And he'd know since after he graduated Charlie stayed on and taught there for almost forty years."

Kitty smiled at Charlie. "That's very sweet."

"And you're just as nice," Charlie spit out. "And if it wasn't for your father, maybe one day she'd have looked my way."

"And when was that, big fella? You see, Kitty, ole Charlie's always been kind of shy. He just admired your mother. Never really said anything to her like that. Then Roosevelt swooped in and snapped her up."

"I waited too long," Uncle Turtle muttered.

"But I hear you're not like that," Ralph continued. "I understand that you say what you need to straight on."

Kitty startled. That was awfully direct but she could appreciate it because what he said was true. Ralph was definitely Lou's brother so she'd better tread lightly. She drew in a deep breath. "I'm known to be direct. So what are your questions about me and Davis?"

Charlie placed a stick-like hand on her shoulder. "You look just like your mother, but I see what you got from your father. Just like him you go after what you want. That's good." He tapped his fingers up and down. "We just want to know if you're going to be good for our boy," he said slowly.

Kitty looked into the watery eyes of a dying man filled with love for his nephew. She squinted to keep the tears from forming in her own. "I'm going to really try," she said, turning to both his uncles. She blinked several times before she spoke again. "Uncle Ralph, I met your wife. Where's your wife, Uncle Charlie?"

Charlie turned his head and sank a bit further into his shell.

"Charlie lost his wife Emma a little over a year ago. Folks still say she was the nicest woman in the county."

Kitty shrank a bit. How could she have forgotten? "I'm so sorry. Of course Davis told me all about his sweet Aunt Emmy."

Uncle Charlie gave a weak but sincere smile. "That's true. God blessed me real good with Emmy."

The soft wide hand of Ralph's wife Mary tapped Kitty's shoulder. "That's enough out of you two. Lou wants me to bring Kitty over to meet the prayer group. Ralph, I think it's time we take Charlie home. Too much of this night air ain't good for him."

Kitty looked back at Mary. Her tight fried hair glistened with bergamot grease. Mary was the plump, jolly pillar of the community, the type that voted for her father because of her mother. The Thorntons were a wonderfully close and functional family. They supported and took care of each other. Davis had told her that Ralph and Mary had effectively moved into Charlie's house to take care of him during his decline.

Ralph stood up to stretch his long legs. The height definitely came from that side of the family. "Naw, Mary. She don't need to go over there for that. Me and Charlie just now getting to know her."

Mary shook her head. "Come on, Kitty. Don't worry, they'll be on their best behavior since the pastor's sitting with them."

She glanced over at the table of women. Lou waved.

Charlie held his hand up, his signal that he had something to say, so they all waited. "You go on, Kitty. She needs to go over there and meet them, Ralph. Lou and Mary's right."

Ralph pushed back his chair. "Hate to lose her but you're right, Brute. She needs to know about that late spring chicken over there with all those ole gossiping hens."

Kitty sucked in her lower lip as she wondered what they meant and what awaited her at that table of Lou's friends.

"Hush, Ralph," Mary tsked.

Ralph winked at her. "We'll send Dave over to save you soon."

She followed Mary to the table of church ladies. It took a few minutes before she realized that the pregnant lady who tsked every time someone asked too personal a question was their pastor. She'd introduced herself as Janelle and had insisted Kitty call her by her first name, which had made Lou and Mary harrumph.

The conversation followed in the same nice nosey vein as every other conversation this weekend. Where'd she meet Davis? How long had they been dating? What were her plans?

After a few minutes Janelle's husband came to the table and insisted they go home, so she could rest.

"No, I'll sit a while longer." Pastor Janelle smiled up at her husband. "I think getting to know Kitty a little bit will help me understand more about who Davis Thornton is."

"Lord have mercy," Lou blew out.

Kitty sucked in her lower lip to remind herself to tread lightly.

"I'm out of here." Pastor's very tall, dark, and handsome husband, James Whitney, shook his head and strode away.

It seemed to Kitty that he knew better than to stay around a hen party. She hoped Davis would come to save her soon. Kitty shifted in her seat and tucked her legs sideways as her mother had taught them to do during press interviews. She took a deep breath to collect her thoughts for more important questioning.

The youngest lady in the klatch spoke up. "Pastor, I'd think everything you need to know was evidenced strongly tonight, when Davis spoke. His speech was so inspiring and thought provoking I think I'm good."

Kitty focused on the woman Uncle Ralph must have been referring to as the late spring chicken among these old hens. The woman looked to be in her mid-thirties, and the admiration in her voice was clear. She was interested in Davis.

"Pastor, you know Davis just preached! I think I'll sleep in tomorrow," the late spring chicken clucked.

The ladies all laughed while Kitty glanced around the room for Davis.

"Sister Terri, I agree, but your Sunday school students might miss you," Pastor Janelle gently admonished with a twinkle in her eye.

Janelle seemed kind, generous, and thoroughly uncomfortable. Kitty didn't want the conversation to venture into the church arena, so she employed one of her father's oldest tricks.

"Pastor Janelle, when's your baby due?" she asked.

"In about two weeks."

After that the conversation shifted into territory Kitty knew little about: pregnancy, childbirth, and motherhood. Kitty smiled politely as the ladies talked.

"Princess, that's my little nickname for her." Lou took charge when the topic seemed exhausted.

She braced herself, sure an attack would come. Lou was probably going to tell these ladies she wasn't mother material. Was she really sitting here thinking about having babies? With Davis?

"Princess, did you enjoy your dinner?" Lou asked.

That was unexpected. "Yes, Mrs. Thornton, the kitchen did a very nice job tonight."

Lou reached over and gave her a one arm hug. "Kitty, if I'm going to call you princess you're going to have to at least call me Lou. I was glad to see you eat something." She turned back to the table. "Poor little thing didn't eat a bite at our house yesterday. And only picked at her breakfast this morning. Ordinarily I would have taken it personally, but she was a little ill."

"Sure, she didn't eat any of your cooking," one of the senior ladies joked.

The conversation went on, balanced between church gossip and little snippets about Davis. It was clear these ladies were Lou's friends. Only Terri Taylor, the youngest woman in the group, tested Kitty's patience. She was an elementary school principal and clearly had a huge crush on Davis. At every mention of his name, Terri made some gushing comment. Kitty tapped her foot. Didn't this woman know who she was? And maybe since Terri's last comment had something to do with getting Davis involved in neighborhood politics, Terri was counting on the fact that she was from out of town. Kitty held her tongue in neutral and pasted on her mother's political wife smile.

A round of "fine jobs" and "congratulations" rang out around the table when Davis joined them. After checking in with Kitty, he asked Terri to dance. The smile that spread across Terri's face spoke volumes. Kitty glanced around the table. By their facial expressions she could tell the ladies were waiting to gauge her reaction. Since she wasn't the type to get upset about her man dancing a fast tune with another woman, there wouldn't be a reaction. Davis had shown her no disrespect. Kitty smiled and focused on the ladies at the table. "The band's very good," she said.

Pastor Janelle and Lou nodded approval. And the conversation went on to questions about life on Capitol Hill.

"Ladies, I'm going to the washroom. Then it's goodnight." Pastor Janelle struggled to stand. "Sister Mary, can you help me get my coat? Lou, can I ask you to get Whit? You'll find him in some corner whispering with his frat brothers. Those men gossip more than any women I know. And Lou, I know you won't take any nonsense when you tell Whit I said it's time to go." She placed one hand on her rounded belly and extended her other toward Kitty. "It was nice chatting with you, Kitty Franklin. I hope to see you in church tomorrow."

Kitty nodded. A weekend with Davis Thornton would of course include attending church. Although he respected her disbelief, this weekend was about her getting to know him better. Attending church was a big part of his life.

After a single set Davis promptly returned Terri to the table and asked for Kitty's hand. She smiled broadly as she excused herself to join him on the dance floor. *Hope Terri Taylor enjoyed that dance 'cause there'll be no more tonight.*

For a big man Davis was light on his feet. He cut a nice step and had a little hip hop flavor in his sway. Since he'd forewarned her, she'd practiced and was prepared to step with him, Chicago-style. They owned the dance floor as other couples admired and attempted to imitate their moves. She smiled as he twirled her again. She liked steppin' with Davis. The dance was social and intimate at the same time. For eight counts he held her close, as if there was no one else on the dance floor. Then he'd spin her out for eight counts and party with the other dancers on the floor.

"Get it, boy," he said to one of his high school friends that danced next to them trying to mimic the Chicago-style steps.

"Step, baby," he'd say to her when he pulled her in close for the next eight counts.

They danced an entire set without stopping. Boppin' and slow draggin'.

"If you're getting hot, why don't you take that little jacket thing off?"

"No, I'm fine."

"Then after our parents are gone," Davis whispered in her ear.

She'd lost all sense of what she wanted to ask him about shift as she reveled in the sensation of being wanted, accepted, and loved in his arms, especially during the slow songs. At the end of the set Davis took a break. She was glad to have a chance to catch her breath. She scanned the almost empty room. Her parents were chatting with the judge and his wife. Lou seemed to be making her way to the door.

Their elders all thought they were moving too fast. But that didn't matter to her. What mattered most was that Davis was kind and honest and had inspired her to shift. She'd had a wonderful weekend with him so far. So what if the relationship was too new for her to be sleeping with him? She usually followed the ninety-day rule. However unconventional this relationship was, it was ripe with promise. What really mattered was that Davis was kind, patient and gentle and being with him felt right.

She hurried across the floor to wish Lou good night.

Chapter 12

Hours later Kitty rolled over and reached out to Davis. Her hand touched only cold bedding. He wasn't where he should have been. "Dave? Davis?" She glanced at the clock. Surely he was home by now. A consistent thumping came from another room in the house. Tired and a bit dizzy, she sat up in bed. When the thumps gave way to a steady bumping, she slipped out of bed and followed the commotion.

"Bullshit," he hissed.

She stood at the door to his den and listened to him hiss and curse under his breath. "Davis?"

"Go back to bed," he growled without looking up from the books he was slamming onto a shelf.

Her brow knitted, "What's wrong?"

"I can't believe you," he blew out.

Kitty rubbed her eyes. "What?"

"Why didn't you tell me that you recommended your father not hire me?" Without looking in her direction, hurt and disappointment spilled from his mouth. "Why?"

She paused for a moment before taking a step into the room. There was no place for her to sit; the room was now in total disarray. Gone were the neat stacks of boxes from this morning. How long had he been home? Now most of the boxes were half empty; their contents littered the floor.

He seemed to be searching for something packed away in one of the boxes. Kitty bit her lip. "I didn't think you'd be happy working for my father."

Davis turned and started sorting through another box. "That's not it," he said and threw some magazines into a recycling bin.

"Davis," she whimpered.

He didn't respond.

"How'd you find out?" She eased further into the room. Her heart raced ahead of her and she reached out for the edge of his desk for support. "He waited until tonight to tell you, didn't he?" She looked down at her bare feet. "I wrote that Thanksgiving night, before I really knew you."

"And you didn't rescind it. Even after you knew how much I wanted this. But that's not it. When were you going to tell me?" he yelled, then threw a book over to a pile near the desk.

She jumped and tried to figure out how to respond. She searched for an argument that might provide her a little wiggle room. "And you purposely kept your hiring from me."

"That's not what this is about." His voice went up another octave.

She tried a classic rebuttal-redirection. "So you lie to me for weeks and that's supposed to be okay?"

"Oh, no, that's not going to work with me, baby," he snapped. "You should have told me this straight up. You think I'm so weak I couldn't take knowing you didn't want me to have this job? All those talks, but no truth."

The intensity in his tone rattled her. Her only defense was to yell, "My daddy—"

"This ain't got nothing to do with your daddy."

He was so loud she thought the windows might rattle.

"It's about you being grown enough to stand on your own word. You aren't woman enough to stand on your own truth. That's the problem. I don't know how they do things where you're from but here," he pointed at his chest, "here that's a problem."

His truth cut her deep. Deep and with a punishing stroke. She should have told him yesterday, got this out in the open. She opened her mouth, but nothing came out.

He continued, "I don't need some lying little daddy's girl that's going to stab me in my back. I need a grown woman that's going to support me and be for me. Be on my side. Even if I didn't get the job, as long as you were honest with me, we'd a been okay." His vocal inflection was strong, dark, and hostile.

"Davis, Davis, please," she whimpered, unable to escape the strength and conviction of his words. His words actually seemed to have power to weaken her.

He kept ranting. "Is it even possible for you to be for me? Or are you that caught up with your father?"

She felt another blow to her core. "Stop! It's not like that. I am for you...."

"Shut up," he murmured in a thick voice. "Shut up." He breathed out yet another soul-penetrating holler. "Shut up."

She inhaled. The air rushed in and burned through her chest. Dread coursed through her body, followed closely by a new and painful sensation. Her knees wobbled.

Davis returned to his boxes and released a heavy snort.

A wave of regret washed over her. He'd said they were no longer okay. Her body contracted. She clung to the edge of the desk and willed her legs to stop trembling. She stood there for a while, silenced by his command. Being bested in a loud, hard-driving, dirty South verbal battle, like gangster rappers' spit, was not how this night was supposed to end.

Davis never turned around. His heavy breathing crowded out any ambient sounds in the room. Another book landed near her feet.

After a few minutes Kitty inched her way back to the bedroom and plopped down at the foot of the bed and wept.

Sometime in the night he must have crept into bed. In the early gray of dawn she awoke and drew close to him.

"Don't touch me," he said.

Kitty backed away. She pulled at the covers and drew her legs up as salty tears wet her lips. He hadn't even turned to look at her. She worried. Things had been going so well between them. Last night had been an almost magical evening. After his speech and photo op, she'd received such a warm Southern reception from his uncles and family friends. Their hugs and kind words filled her heart. Even Lou had said nice things about her. Then he had to go smoke that celebratory cigar with her father. *Damn you, Daddy!*

She'd been too happy to comprehend his expression when he told her that Glynnis would drive her home. He'd made some excuse about having to stay and make sure everything was properly locked up. Now she remembered the way he'd scowled when she told him he could trust Penny, the Center's maintenance chief. He'd kind of turned away from her then and mumbled that he'd see her at home.

Less than an hour later Davis rolled out of bed. "I'm going for a run. Then we're going to eight o'clock service, so you might want to start getting ready soon." He stomped out of the room.

※

They didn't speak much on the way to church. His mood was so different, unfamiliar. Well, in truth she hadn't known him long enough to know all of his ways and moods. Mama Cat was right. She'd moved too fast and had made a mistake. Kitty turned to look at the large, brooding man as he turned into the church's parking lot and pulled into a parking space next to the building. The placeholder read DEACON THORNTON.

"This is Uncle Charlie's spot. He's no longer driving, so he said I could park here this weekend."

Kitty nodded and placed her hand on the door handle.

"Wait a minute." He turned toward her and looked over her head. "I'll come around and get the door for you. And let's keep our business in our house."

He hadn't given her as much as a passing glance since they left his house and now he was asking her to put on a happy face. She searched his face when he opened the door for her. His expression reminded her of one of her father's. For the first time she thought that her father and Davis might have something in common. *If he thinks for one minute that I'm like my mother, then he doesn't know me.* Worry and dread over his saying they were no longer all right collided with his request and stirred a quake.

When she stepped into the sanctuary the headache intensified. But she smiled her way through a dozen introductions and was glad when they were able to sit down. The usher escorted them to the second row and seated them next to her parents.

She glanced around. This had to be the biggest church in Rock Hill now. She hadn't been here since the last campaign cycle, and that was before the construction was completed on the new sanctuary. The small, traditional Baptist Methodist Assembly Church her mother joined when she moved back to Rock Hill seven years ago now convened in a modern mega-church facility.

It had been years since she'd attended church as a regular worshipper. Most of her church visits were campaign stops, the kind where she sat and waited for the pastor to recognize her. Then she'd give some rousing remarks about the candidate, sit back down, and wait for the choir to sing so she could get on to the next stop. She'd stopped going to church for worship when she began to believe there was no redemption for the wrongs she'd covered up for her father.

Kitty hadn't heard a sermon for years and, with the growing ache in her head, she knew she was certain not to hear one this morning. Not that preaching could change anything in her life. There wasn't room in her brain for another sermon anyway. She'd been fully convicted by the sermon Davis yelled at her last night about standing on the truth.

They sat as a couple, but not close. Davis was polite, but she could tell by the stiffness in his back that he was still angry. She shifted her attention to her parents. They sat in the same way. Together, but not close. This wasn't what she wanted in a relationship.

Her mother was impeccably dressed, as always, with the perfect winter white pillbox hat and matching gloves. Yesenia clapped her gloved hands while the congressman stood up to be recognized as a special guest.

Pastor Janelle asked her father to be ever mindful of the poor and said she'd pray for his continued wisdom. "I'm not quite sure, church, how to recognize another one of our special visitors." Pastor Janelle paused briefly and placed her hand on her protruding belly. Her liturgical robe lay open over her black maternity dress. "I think I'll just say this. I'd like to welcome Catherine Franklin, who is also worshipping with us this morning."

Kitty gave an appreciative nod for not introducing her as somebody's daughter or girlfriend. The look Lou shot Davis from the choir said that it wasn't the intro she would have preferred. Kitty stared down at her feet. Davis was right about needing a woman who would stand on her own truths.

In recent years truth for her had been muddled. And she had stopped considering questions of truth for herself. When it came to her father she was like most partisans. Right and wrong didn't matter. What mattered was which side of the issue her father stood on. Her father paid her handsomely to use the law to bend his wrongs into rights. Whether it was accepting gifts from lobbyists or cleaning up after a personal indiscretion, Kitty found the words to justify her father's behavior so he could appear faultless before the public. And she did it because she loved him. Then along came Davis, who asked only for the simple truth. She was confused and afraid that she didn't know what the simple truth was anymore. She glanced over at her mother and wondered what truths Yesenia stood on. As the service continued, the throb in her head kept pace with the spirit-filled singing and testimonial shouting. Midway through the sermon, Davis stretched out and placed his arm behind her head on the pew. Kitty shifted position and he immediately took his arm down.

By the end of the service, Kitty was totally uncomfortable with Davis sitting on her left with his heart beyond her reach. They needed to talk. Maybe she could explain why she didn't tell him she'd recommended against his hire. Maybe he'd understand and help her shift. Then they'd be all right again. She was so nervous about the state of their relationship she squirmed and fidgeted like a little girl. The simple truth was that she was in love with Davis.

Kitty looked at her father sitting next to her. He seemed almost carefree in the face of his ever-present problems. Her knees wobbled.

She wanted to leave as soon as Pastor Janelle spoke the benediction, but Davis insisted that she do the right thing. So she smiled and wished everyone good day. While her headache raged, she shook hands and hugged his uncles and congratulated the pastor on an inspiring sermon. She put on her mother's persona and met more of the church family. The act went well until Lou took center stage.

"What's wrong, Princess?" Lou asked, still wearing her choir robe.

In true Franklin family fashion, Kitty blasted Lou a ninety mega-watt smile. "Oh, I'm fine."

Lou frowned. "You're just getting to know me, so you don't know yet that I'm not one for pretense. You can paste on that smile for everyone else, but I see right through it. Your head is hurting you again this morning. I could tell by the way you never looked up during the sermon. I want you to go lie down." Lou paused and studied her face. "Don't you think you need to see your doctor? Two migraines in one weekend? That's not normal for you, is it?"

"No, ma'am," she sighed.

Lou reached out and hugged her. "Princess, you go sit down and I'll go tell my boy to take you home." Lou released her and moved over to the right side of the sanctuary where the uncles were giving Davis a tour of the deacons' seats.

Davis slumped down against the wall of his bedroom. There were still a few hours of daylight, and there was so much he wanted to do. He'd planned for Kitty to be with him at the family dinner, then go to the movies together afterward. Instead, he'd dropped her off before he went to Lou's to give her some space. They'd had part two of their argument in the car after church. He'd lost all patience with her when she complained about another headache. He'd yelled something nasty and out of character about her being a sickly little girl.

He regretted those words as soon as he pulled away from his house and he didn't think he could feel worse until he talked to Uncle Charlie. His uncle didn't have much time left on earth, but instead of complaining about his health, his concerns were for Kitty. At his uncle's urging he ate quickly and went home.

They should have had another happy day together. Instead, he was sulking, wondering if their relationship might be over. For the past two weeks he'd told himself that she was too good for him. Too pretty, too accomplished. Women like her didn't usually go for him. Then she'd call and make him feel worthy.

He replayed Friday's conversation with his uncles. He couldn't have imagined Friday afternoon that he'd do exactly what his uncles had warned him against. He'd made Kitty cry. Twice. You've messed up now, and when she tells her daddy how you yelled at her, you'll lose your job. Getting fired after a day on the job will stain your reputation, reason warned. Davis groaned.

She stirred.

He stretched out his legs. "Kitty?" He spoke into the dim room, praying she'd respond.

"Umm-hum."

"Can I get you anything? Do you want to talk?"

"Not if you're going to yell at me," she said in a ragged, broken voice. She stared up at the ceiling.

"I was angry." He paused. "And I apologize for being too loud in the car. My heavy voice can come across as too intense in close quarters."

"Your words really hurt me."

He covered his face with his hands. "I'm sorry. I realize now that you're more sensitive than you let on."

She whimpered.

He'd made her cry again.

"I thought I could be myself with you. I want to be myself with you. But you wouldn't listen to me. And when I asked you to stop, pleaded with you, told you, you were hurting me, you told me to shut up, shut up, shut up." Kitty rolled over and turned her back to him. "I don't want to lose my voice, as my mother has."

She'd stunned him. He sat in silence as his mind raced.

As the sun set, a short physical distance and huge emotional chasm lay between them.

Chapter 13

Kitty stared at the bare wall. Davis hadn't been in this house long enough to hang any pictures in his room. This room Mama Cat said she had no business sleeping in. Grandma's old-fashioned wisdom had been right, again. And she could never tell her family what happened. They didn't need to know her weak spot. Somehow in a short time Davis had gained access to her soul. He'd discovered her closely guarded secret. She was sensitive. Of course she could take angry words. She's heard them often from her sisters and father. Hell, she'd used them in court and with anyone on Capitol Hill who tried to take her father down. But with Davis she'd felt so secure and accepted—until he told her to shut up. It was as if he didn't want her to fully express herself. As a young child who was small she'd quickly learned to use her voice to command attention. As an attorney and negotiator her voice was the source of her power. Her greatest fear was losing her voice, both literally and figuratively.

"In church you treated me like I was a cover girl," she said softly. "I'm not the kind of girl you can yell at and tell shut up, then expect a happy face in public. I did it today so I wouldn't embarrass you, and I don't like how it felt."

He sat like a stone against the wall.

Beneath the thick comforter she felt an isolating cold. "I didn't know you well enough to be here," she sobbed. Her whole being hurt, inside and out. She'd had failed love affairs before, but this hurt was different. This hurt impacted her resolve. She needed to get up and leave, but couldn't summon the energy. Just like the night she'd met him, deep down she didn't want to go. She wasn't ready to leave him, or for this relationship to be over.

She stewed for a while, then worked up the moxy to raise up on one elbow. She plopped back down. Anger crept in. This wasn't like her. Her head throbbed and her heart pounded in her ears. She glanced over to where Davis still sat on the floor.

"Kitty," he called out. "My mother sent you some soup. You really need to eat something."

His soft tones reminded her of how kind he'd been the night they met. How he'd made her feel so safe and warm, as if she'd been with him for ages.

"Okay."

He left the room and she willed herself out of bed. She decided to take a shower and let the water run while she dried off, knowing Davis wouldn't be likely to come in until the water stopped.

There was no one she could turn to for support, not even her mother. She'd have to bear this hurt alone? Yesenia had a cardinal rule regarding relationships. She always said, 'If you want your family to respect your man, don't tell them anything negative about him.' Their mother encouraged all of her girls to refrain from the man-bashing conversations that were common among girlfriends.

The last time she'd had her heart broken she'd gone to Twanna. After cheesecake and sympathy, in the end things wound up just the way her mother always taught. When she made up with her ex she couldn't stand to be around Tee. Not after the tell-all. The man was a highly regarded naval officer, but he'd lost all respect in Twanna's eyes and the reconciliation didn't last.

From her luggage she pulled on a plus-sized family reunion tee shirt. She focused for a moment on her father's branch. Her mother had insisted that Reggie, Yvette, and Quanny be listed in their proper place. 'They all are and always will be family,' her mother still said. No matter what Dr. Reggie did or failed to do concerning Quanny, her mother refused to allow Yvette to discuss those negative aspects of the relationship. Now Kitty understood the wisdom of her mother's advice.

If any good could come out of this situation she vowed to never disparage her sister again for putting up with Reggie's mess for Quanny's sake. She'd even be cordial to Reggie's wife. Maybe she was more like her mother than she thought?

About ten minutes after she returned to bed, he knocked. On her signal he brought in a bed tray with a red rose in a small vase. He also turned on a table lamp, since the day was done.

"Turkey soup. Mama cooked turkey for Sunday dinner. She said she's gonna put your name on the prayer list for this evening's service."

Her eyes crossed.

"She assumed it was just the headache."

Kitty nodded and picked up the spoon. She didn't have the strength to curse him for using one of her father's favorite political tricks. Never correct an assumption made in your favor. For the second time today she recognized a similarity between Davis and her father, and she didn't like it.

"Can I stay? Are you willing to talk?" he asked.

"It's your house."

"No, it's your call. And if you ask me to, I'll go sleep at my mother's tonight."

She looked over at him and hesitated. The same man who left his hotel room so she would be comfortable showering and dressing was willing to leave his own house to make her comfortable. His kindness would be her undoing. "Stay."

He sat at the edge of the bed as she spooned up some of the steaming comfort.

"Penny for your thoughts, counselor?"

"Cat's finally got my tongue, Mr. Thornton."

He broached a tentative smile. "I honestly don't want to remember anything about last night other than the pleasure of having you beside me throughout the evening."

She coughed. A bit of fire flashed in her eyes.

He put up his palms. "Wait, baby, hear me out. I said some things in the heat of the moment that I'm regretting."

She nodded and took another bit of the simple soup, just meat broth, celery, and a little rice; it was the best thing Lou had made all weekend.

"Kitty, I'm a man who takes responsibility for his actions. I apologize for the yelling. It's killing me that this is happening now, with you."

"You're worried I'm going to say something to my father?"

His head hung low.

"Kitty, you need to know that your father has been very clear about what's going to happen to me if I hurt you."

"I'm not telling him anything."

He coughed.

"I'm not telling my mother, either," she hissed.

"Thank you. Honestly, that had crossed my mind."

She moved the tray and swung her legs to the side of the bed. "Then you don't know my mother. I can't talk to her. She has this thing. She doesn't like to talk about relationships, hers or other people's. She says a relationship is between two people."

Davis stood and picked up the tray. "I'm going to move this before it gets upset. Your mother is right, and that's all I meant this morning. I wasn't asking you to be a cover girl, as you called it. I was just asking that you keep our business in our house." He sat the tray on the dresser. "Kitty, I don't understand something. If you don't talk to your mother, then do you and your sisters talk?"

"No."

"Then how did you know about Quanny's father? How'd you know that he was engaged before your sister? And that report you threatened Dena with? How do you know about what's going on with them if you don't talk?"

"Daddy," she said flatly.

"You have a very complex relationship with your father, and I don't know where that leaves your sisters or me."

He picked up the tray and left the room for the night.

Kitty stood in the doorway of the kitchen and watched Davis at the makeshift breakfast table. Bright and early Monday morning and he was ready for work. He'd given her more space than she'd wanted last night. Today was his first full day at the Center. They should be celebrating. If things had been different, maybe she would have gotten up early and made him breakfast.

His starched white shirt stretched across his broad back, and his red and navy striped necktie hung over his shoulder as he ate. She inhaled his fresh scent. She cracked half a smile. He had been so cute tiptoeing around this morning when he came in to get his stuff out of the bedroom.

When he went out for his run earlier, she'd used the time to dress and pack her things. She teetered on her heels and stepped into the kitchen.

"Can you call a cab to take me to my mother's house?"

He looked up from his cereal bowl. "I'll take you. I have to go over anyway. I have a meeting with your father before he leaves."

"I'm ready to leave now. I don't want… " she started and rubbed her eyes.

"That doesn't make any sense, Kitty. I'll take you. Unless," he stood, "unless you're planning on throwing a tantrum like you did on Thanksgiving."

"No." She hung her head and went into the living room to wait. Why did he have to keep reminding her that she was a little girl and he wanted a grown woman?

She stared out of the window at the neat houses and small stores that stood between Davis's home and her mother's house. Several years ago one of the first stories of the twenty-four-hour news cycle was her father's affair with a junior congresswoman from Illinois. That scandal, combined with the advent of paparazzi-style stalking of politicians, ran her mother out of DC.

Yesenia's move came as a total surprise to the family. It was the first time in acknowledged history that Yesenia had stood up for herself. It was also one of the few times they could recall hearing their parents argue. Kitty was so proud of her mother that she represented her at the property closing, a move her father did not appreciate. At the closing Yesenia presented a cashier's check for the full purchase price of the house. When Kitty recovered from the shock, her mother explained that over the years she'd secretly kept a sunshine fund. In a rare moment Yesenia advised Kitty to start one if she ever married.

Davis parked his car in front of her mother's two-story Colonial hideout. When she bought the house it was in a marginal part of town. But gentrification had come and now Yesenia Franklin's home was the jewel of Rock Hill's historic district.

"You go ahead, Kitty. I'll bring up your luggage."

She scanned the street for any remnants of the press that reportedly crowded the block over the weekend. Only one battered Ford Escort parked across the street, a die-hard pappi. She took a deep breath. When she checked the blogosphere last night there was already some chatter about her being with Davis at the Christmas party. Now there would be another picture of them for sale, probably to her father's opponent in the upcoming election. "So this is it. Goodbye."

Davis placed his arm on the passenger's side headrest and turned to face her. "I hope not. I hope we can find our way together."

"What does that mean, Davis?"

"I can't explain it, but you know how much I really like you. But I'm going to wait for you to make the next move."

She couldn't turn her face to look at him. Kitty nodded and opened the door. Slowly, she made her way up the six steep steps. As soon as she stepped onto the porch the front door swung open and her father filled the entry space.

Her eyes narrowed. Knowing him, he'd watched them from the porthole in the front door. "Daddy?"

"Morning, Kitty. Your mother and grandmother are in the parlor."

She recognized her cue to exit. She steadied her gaze on her father's face. His brows were creased. He was angry about something.

"You can just leave those on the porch, Davis. The driver can pick them up from there," Roosevelt bellowed and turned to walk into the house.

Kitty and Davis moved into the house behind her father. Kitty stood between the two men. An uncomfortable silence settled around them.

"Did you have a nice weekend, Kitten?"

She forced a smile. "Yes, Daddy."

Roosevelt's creased brow eased. He looked over her head. "Did you take the time to sign those contracts, Davis? You don't go on the payroll until we get that done. Even if that was the best Christmas party we've ever thrown." Roosevelt exhaled and grinned.

"Thank you, sir. I'm glad you were pleased, but the credit is due to Glynnis. I haven't found the time to review the contracts yet."

The older man scowled.

Kitty put her hands on her hips and glowered at her father. "What contracts? You didn't ask me to generate any contracts for Davis." She drew in a sharp breath and anger flashed in her eyes. "And I know why. Daddy, don't mess over Davis." She turned to the man behind her. "Don't sign anything until you've had your own attorney review it."

"Hold up, counselor, you're my attorney," Roosevelt chortled.

Davis cracked a half smile. "Thank you, lady."

"Well, goodbye, Davis."

He reached out for her. "Remember what I said." The strength and conviction in his voice filled the hall.

She took a few steps forward. Between her father and Davis, she wobbled. Neither man reached out to help her. An odd sensation filled her chest. She was caught in a strange no-man's land. No longer Daddy's baby and no longer Davis's lady. She steadied herself with the wall and drew on her inner strength as a woman on her own. She took another step in her father's direction. Concern again deepened his brow. She pasted on her little girl smile. "Daddy, can I get a wheelchair at the airport? I have a headache."

"Of course, Kitten." His face darkened.

As she moved to the back of the house, she shuddered at the coldness of her reality. Neither of them could help her make the important decisions ahead.

Kitty paused in the hall and attempted to pull herself together before she entered the private domain of her mother, where nothing negative about her man could be said.

"Hey, baby."

Mama Cat's greeting sent her straight to her grandmother's arms. She collapsed at the elderly woman's knees.

While Mama Cat consoled her, her mother clucked. "Kitty, say it isn't so. We were just saying how wonderful it would be if things worked out between you and Davis."

Kitty inhaled deeply and stood up to face her mother. Her older mirror image smiled sweetly.

"Sit down and have something to eat. It will help you feel better."

As she rounded the table Kitty took special notice of her mother's disappointed expression as Yesenia filled a plate with biscuits and scrambled eggs from the sideboard. Kitty reached out for the food her mother offered. There was nothing in this world like her mother's homemade biscuits. Her father called his favorite breakfast honey and heaven. But food wasn't what she needed most. It was a compassionate listening ear, which she wasn't going to get.

"If you girls would just slow down and wait, let a man court you properly," her grandmother mused.

Kitty's head popped up from her plate. Anybody else and she'd unleash her tongue.

"I just think things might work out better. That's all I'm saying," Mama Cat finished.

Kitty's head lowered. Mama Cat was right. She should have taken her grandmother's advice and spent the weekend in this house and let Davis come to call, as Mama Cat put it. But that wouldn't have stopped their argument. What she really should have done was keep Davis away from her father. But that wasn't the answer either. All she'd really needed to do was tell Davis the truth.

Her mother took a seat at the table. "And speaking of that, Kitty, please don't be vindictive. Even though it didn't work out between the two of you, it shouldn't cost the man his job."

"Oh," the older lady patted her lap. "I hadn't though about that. 'Member what Rosey did to the last one that broke his kitten's heart."

Kitty closed her eyes briefly. Her last serious boyfriend was a special assistant to the Undersecretary of the navy. When he cheated on her, Roosevelt had used his influence to have that brother reassigned to a naval post in northern Alaska. Her lips formed a circle. She should never have told Twanna anything. As much as she loved Tee, sometimes she regretted hiring her away from Daddy. Those two still had a bond.

"Ump, ump, ump. What a shame." Her grandmother pushed her wheelchair back from the table. "That's one fine young man. And I'm not being fresh. That boy is fine inside and out, got me about make a change, or shift, as he put it the other night. And daughter, if you're going to be in town Sunday, I might go to church with you."

"Mama, you're just talking. You know I'm going to Washington for the congressional Christmas party." Yesenia laughed.

"You caught that quick," Mama Cat shot back. "But that man, whew!"

"He isn't perfect," Kitty spit out.

A disapproving scowl crossed her mother's face.

Mama Cat pulled her shawl closer around her shoulders. "Ain't none of 'em. And if you don't want him, that Terri Tyler Texas does."

She looked up. "What do you know about her? And her name was Terri Taylor. She's from Tyler, Texas."

"Well, you'd have forgot how all those T's went together if you'd seen how her face lit up when Davis introduced her to me the other night. That's what I meant to say to you Saturday. She was there early, that Terri, right when the reception started, all up in the man's face. So I wheeled myself over."

For Mama Cat to take notice and repeat that sort of detail could only mean one thing. She liked Davis, too.

Yesenia waved her hand. "Come to think of it, Mama, you're right. Terri's on the scholarship committee with me, and she's been very happy about Davis moving back here. She's become good friends with the Thornton family."

"Bet she thought she was telling you something at that last meeting when she announced Davis purchased a house near hers." Mama Cat pursed her lips and tsked. "And I bet my last nickel she thinks that man is all right."

There'd been more talk about Davis in this house than she realized. "Then there are some things she doesn't know," Kitty roared back.

Her mother and grandmother's necks snapped back in unison. Mama Cat's eyes rolled up to the ceiling. Her face twisted into her infamous, 'Lord help this child' expression, the one she'd used before she disciplined them as children.

Yesenia stood and poured herself another cup of coffee. "And we don't need to know." She spoke quietly, as if to the wind. "No one else needs to know." Her voice returned to its normal octave. "A relationship is what two people agree upon." Yesenia sat and pondered her cup. From her intense gaze it appeared as if she were reading tea leaves, or at least the coffee grounds.

Kitty studied her now-cold eggs. Another relationship she would never understand, these two. Mama Cat, the woman who put her husband out, no questions asked, no turning back, when she caught him coming out of the Rock Hill movie house holding another woman's hand. Daddy's problem might just be genetic.

She stole a glance at her beloved grandmother, who appeared to be deep in prayer, then to her mother, still staring deeply into her cup. Yesenia had accepted an extraordinary amount of mess from her husband, and in the process she'd lost the respect of her daughters.

"Kitty, go wash your face and get yourself together. The car will be here shortly, and we don't need for your father to know you've been crying."

Chapter 14

Kitty kicked the covers off the twin bed she'd slept in since she was a teen. She wasn't a six-year-old who needed to be sent to her room for a nap. As a consequence of her weekend headaches her parents had insisted she come home and rest for a few days before she re-entered the bustle of District life. She lifted the computer away from her thighs. In some ways she was glad her mother was home to take care of her. She was still weary from the weekend and trying to process Davis's challenge that she stand on her own truth. Plus, she was sick of reviewing the legal brief she needed to finish.

"I'll call when I'm done," she yelled at her chirping phone. Over the course of two days, Davis had bombarded her with dozens of emails and text messages. He'd also sent flowers. She looked over at the bouquet of red roses and the basket of floral greens and jessamine that Twanna had hand-delivered a few hours ago.

"What to do?" She sighed. She knew. "Get up, girlfriend."

It was time to recover. After two days of drug-induced sleep and one long night of contemplation, there was work to do and a decision to make. She could deal with tough discussion, arguments, and a little yelling, but Davis's words had cut straight through her. His 'shut up, shut up, shut up' had wounded her spirit.

She thought back to the way he'd cared for her the night they met. Davis had been the epitome of genuine honesty and goodness. Her shoulders slumped. Despite the fact that their relationship was new, there was more between them than that nasty argument. They had a connection. He cared for her, and she was wrong for not telling him the entire truth. Yet he still hoped they could find their way together. It was what she wanted, too. She picked up her phone and called him. Glynnis said he was in a meeting, so she sent him a text. To be perfectly clear she abandoned the standard text abbreviations.

WHAT DO WE DO NEXT?

Frustrated, she threw the BlackBerry across the room. The device landed in her closet and sank into a pile of old clothes. Was she just like her mother? Could she bury this unpleasant episode with Davis the way she just covered her phone? She grabbed her highlighter and focused all of her energy on the fifth draft of the child support agreement she had to finish. Twanna needed to get this back in the morning at the latest so that all parties involved could prepare for the settlement conference.

She reviewed the non-disclosure clause, which said no interviews, no book deals, no media contact of any kind, including giving testimony in church, until such time as the congressman retired. She chewed the end cap of the marking pen. That wasn't quite tight enough. It wouldn't be enough to keep the secret until the congressman retired. It must be kept until... She turned the pen around. Wrote d-e-, then stopped. She couldn't write the word 'death' associated with her father.

To refocus, she flipped to the section regarding the financial settlement. Here she reached a point of detachment in the legal language of pursuant, petition, and surety. She chewed on the end of a pencil. The financial settlement wasn't that difficult to draft. Somehow her father had come up with the Georgetown tuition. There really wasn't much more left to do. Through the Congressional Black Caucus Foundation, her father's son had just been awarded a full scholarship to Georgetown. All she had to do was increase the amount of the monthly stipend that her father was already paying and file for an extension of the health insurance he was providing.

"Amazing," she muttered. Her father had essentially negotiated and set this up without her knowledge. Now all he needed her to do was apply some legalese to cover the simple truth. He'd been unfaithful to his wife, fathered a child out of wedlock, and had done some influence peddling to get the scholarship. But as she reviewed the brief on her computer, it didn't look as if her father had done anything wrong. When she printed this, it would be a series of expertly presented words on legal paper. No right or wrong, no hurt or injury. Just words on a paper, black and white.

The be-bop of her ringtone, "Mr. Fantastic," reconnected her to reality. She froze. It would be impossible for her to find that phone under the pile of clothes before it went to voice mail. But two days of not hearing

Davis's smooth baritone live and in real time was too long. She leaped toward the closet and fell over her suitcase. A sharp pain pierced her thigh. She whimpered as the ring tone went silent.

Long after her phone went to voice mail, she sat staring out her bedroom window at the Washington Monument. Did her reliance on the obelisk begin before she moved into this room, or did she choose this room for the view? She picked this room for its view, she realized. When she was ten, being able to see the Monument helped her feel closer to her father when he worked late on Capitol Hill. Now the great stone gave her perspective. Her problems were not insurmountable.

She reached up to run her fingers through her hair. The ruby ring her parents gave her when she graduated from law school stuck in the still-tight mass of crunchy curls. It was time to get up and wash her hair. She gathered her papers and set them aside, then retrieved her phone and sent a text to Twanna.

MAKE ME AN APPTMNT WITH THAT CRAZY CUT STYLIST OF YOURS.

If she was going to be like her mother, she certainly didn't have to look just like her, too.

An hour later Kitty tiptoed downstairs, lured by the scent of her mother's cooking. Yesenia was making one of her favorites, chicken paprikash. The aromas of garlic and paprika hung in the air. She stopped just before she passed the opening of her father's study. She wanted to cross that entrance strong. Even after the restorative power of a long, hot shower, her gait was still a little off. She'd bruised her thigh when she fell and it still stung. She cringed at the boom in her father's voice.

"Your work is not at issue, it's your job that's in jeopardy," he yelled.

Who had incurred his wrath?

Most lobbyists and politicians on both sides of the aisle had long since learned not to anger Congressman Franklin. His seniority and connections could quickly dismantle a career. She was curious, and as her father's attorney she didn't have to eavesdrop. She stepped into the office.

"If my Kitten sheds one more tear, Yesenia won't be able to stop me from…"

Her mouth dropped. "Daddy, stop it. Don't talk to Davis like that."

Her father stood behind his massive oak desk and glowered at her. He hissed into the phone, "I'm done with you on that matter, but with regard to the other, we want your first quarter plans and financial projections by the end of the week." He slammed the phone down. "Umm, young lady you don't interfere when I'm talking man-to-man with Davis or anybody else." He pointed a stubby dark finger at her. "You're taking sides against me?"

"This isn't a political contest. And you have no right to speak to Davis about our relationship. That's between the two of us." She took two uneven steps forward and came to a quick stop. "I mean it. Stay out of our business."

"Stop trying to defend him." He plopped down in his oversized leather chair. His meaty hands landed on his desk and scattered some papers. "I can't stand to see you hurting."

Her stomach churned. "My God, Daddy, you've asked me to represent you in a paternity suit. It's you that's hurting me. You have a son." She ran across the room to the private bath and threw up.

"That has nothing to do with how much I love you," he yelled at her back.

She hugged the toilet bowl and threw up again.

It took her hours to recover from her encounter with her father. Her mother sat with her. Yesenia, as usual, didn't say much or ask any questions about the argument with her father. Her mother did acknowledge that she was upset about Davis, but wouldn't hear any details. What Kitty really needed was someone she could talk to about what had happened and have that person explain to her why she wanted him so badly. All her mother did was pump her full of comfort food and a dose of prescription drugs.

It was late but she dialed Davis anyway. Their conversation was strained. They talked about his day and the weather in DC She smiled when he asked if she'd been able to catch a glimpse of her Monument.

"Tell me what you worked on today," he asked, just to keep the conversation going.

"Bunch of junk, mostly." She paused. "There is one thing that I want to ask you about."

"Shoot."

"You know one of the things I do is monitor the media. Websites, blogs, Facebook postings, tweets…"

"I think I know where this is leading. Jackie was doing a little research about my new job and came across a few sites and blogs."

"Was removeRooseveltFranklin.com one of those sites?"

"Yes, that site in particular has some seriously negative things to say about your father." He drew in a sharp breath.

"I've been monitoring it closely and think it's time to shut it down. But…"

"Spit it out, lady."

"Do you own the email address thorninyourside@hotmail.com?"

"Yes."

"And your mother is thornyone@comcast.net?" Kitty smiled; that Lou was something else. "And CaptainJackThorn@comcast.net is Jackie and MrsAnders85 is Sharon," she continued.

"There's got to be more people than just my family reading that blog."

"There are. Terri Taylor logged in and posted a comment over the weekend. She actually uses her full name in her email address. Not very savvy." She covered her mouth with her hand. That had come out with a bit too much attitude.

"Wait a minute. How is it that you can tell who is reading that blog?" he asked.

"Twanna. My girl is a computer whiz, but she can't seem to figure out who owns this site. Although I suspect it's owned by my father's real opponent in the upcoming primary."

"Whoever owns that blog seems determined to discredit your father. I'm actually glad you brought this up. I didn't like seeing that a picture of us from Saturday night was posted before we made it to church on Sunday morning."

"I know, but did you notice how quickly that was pushed aside? The moderator actually made a decent comment when he posted that we're not in the public eye."

"Yea, but then black-neo-con lambasted your father's family values with comments about how he uses you."

She groaned.

"Kitty, I'm going to speak to my family. They'll stop posting. But what about the other people who read and post?"

"It's a free country, but I'm going to find out who they are. And if any of them work for my father in DC or at the Center, they've crossed the line. I'll take care of them."

"Oooh," he bristled. "You sound as intense as your father. I'll do a little checking around, make sure no one here is fueling the fires."

There was silence on the line. She didn't know what to say next. Even though she knew he was the only person she could or should talk to about her feelings.

"Now, Kitty, what about us?"

She lowered the phone to rest on her breast for a minute. Then she lifted the receiver and snapped, "I'm not sure, yet."

"Whoo-hoo." He let out a nervous-sounding laugh. "Am I close to being forgiven, since you're snapping at me?"

"Don't laugh at me," she exhaled. "I'm afraid."

He drew in a sharp breath. "I don't like the sound of that at all. I'm so sorry I've caused you to be afraid of me."

"I'm not afraid of you. I'm afraid of becoming like my mother." Her confession came out in a still, small voice.

"That's deep. I wouldn't know how to touch that."

She took a deep breath. Her relationship with both her parents was inexplicable. "Davis, how do you feel about me?"

"I don't want to skew anything here by talking about my feelings."

"But?"

"No buts, listen to me. What's important is, can you forgive me? Without forgiveness of faults big and small our relationship can't survive. Without forgiveness, love doesn't matter."

Kitty stared out her window. "I've never thought about it like that." Her mind raced. "Did you say that forgiveness is more important than love?"

"I want you to consider carefully what I'm saying. I'm asking for your forgiveness, true forgiveness."

"And I'm just supposed to forget what happened?"

"No, baby, not forget, but to forgive me as I've forgiven you." He spoke in a low, steady tone.

She wanted to say more but, for once, decided to wait, to think carefully before she spoke. Maybe she was shifting. She exhaled just to let him know she was still on the line. This was a radical concept, forgiveness more important than love. "But if you don't love me, why is it even important?"

"Kitty, you know damn well how I feel."

Her kind, considerate, gentle Davis sounded impatient. Had she pushed him too far? Had she made him wait too long? Surely he could give her more than two days to decide. What if she was about to lose him? Wasn't it a simple thing to do, say she forgave him? She sat back on her bed. "After I forgive you, what else would you need from me?"

"Wow, that's a good question because there is something else, although I don't feel like I'm in any position to ask any more of you."

"Tell me."

"There is something about you that I need to decide if I can accept."

The room went cold. She'd never had a relationship discussion like this. Something he needed to decide if he could accept? "Not change?"

"No, Kitty, accept. I'm not trying to ask you to change."

She stood up and paced the room. "You can't ask me to forsake my father," flew out of her mouth.

"No, but now make that two things. I'll have to learn to accept the relationship you have with your father, with both of your parents." He paused. "Kitty, I have to tell you I have a problem with…"

"The fact that I don't believe in God?" She held her breath. Surely that would be a sticky point in the relationship.

"Naw, I'm not worried about that." He laughed.

She bristled. "I don't see what's funny." The more time she spent with Davis the more she had niggling doubts about having turned her back on her faith.

He spoke again with caution, slowly, as he had during his speech Saturday night. "Woman, can you let me talk?"

"Okay." She remembered Yvette's suggestion and zipped her lip.

"I have a problem with your mouth." He paused to let his words resonate. "But I'm not going to ask you to shift that. I've got to figure out if I can put up with it. We have to decide if we can put up with each other."

Was it this simple? Forgiveness and an acknowledgment that neither of them was perfect? Just a simple decision they both needed to make. Could they accept each other?

"Because a relationship is what two people agree to accept in each other?" she repeated one of her mother's favorite phrases. *Oh, God, I'm my mother.*

"Something a lot like that. Uncle Charlie smoked, Aunt Emmy didn't like it. But she accepted it and they lived a long, happy life together. Kitty, I know I have my faults. I'm just praying you'll accept my shortcomings."

"I see," she stuttered. "You've given me a lot to think about, and now my head hurts a little."

"Didn't mean to do that," he murmured in his usual loving, patient tone.

"No, it's not a quake," she added quickly. "It's just you put something heavy on my mind and I want to sit and think about it. I'll be up all night thinking about it. And Davis, I want to be up all night thinking about it. But I need to go right now."

"What else you got to do this time of night?" He sounded slightly worried. "You know I'll stay up with you, use all my minutes for the month if I've got half a chance of making things right with you."

She chuckled. "I'm getting off the phone now because I'm suddenly hungry."

"If you were home with me I'd cook for you."

"Umm." She glanced out her window at the Washington Monument. The gleaming white stone gave her the reassurance she required. "Well, we might as well discuss this now. You know I can't cook, right?"

"I'm willing to accept that."

Her mouth turned into a smile. "I love you, but I'm going to go. My mother made chicken paprikash tonight for me. It's my favorite, and it's time for some more."

"That sounds good, Kitty. Maybe I'll have the chance to eat some more of your mother's good cooking one day." He sounded a little down.

Two plates of chicken later Kitty sat in her mother's kitchen contemplating forgiveness. After years of wondering, she now thought she knew the secret of her parents' marriage. It had to be forgiveness.

"Oh, my God, my mother's a saint."

Only a true saint of God could have accepted the constant affairs and their aftermaths. Wow, the reason she'd met Davis was because of her father's latest affair. It took her a minute to figure it out, but now she knew that her mother was the reason her father hired Davis. Could forgiveness be the power her mother so gracefully wielded? Why her mother never seemed to complain? Because she practiced radical and continual forgiveness for injustices great and small?

Forgiveness was one thing, but acceptance another. There were some things she was unwilling to accept in a relationship, like infidelity. Why had her mother stayed? Maybe her mother was praying for the day when her father would change. Shift, as Davis called it.

"That's not bloody likely." She'd spent her day trying to craft a legal settlement because of another infidelity. "And why I stopped praying years ago." *I can't be forgiven for the things I've done for Daddy by God or Mommy.* She placed her empty plate in the sink and turned off the kitchen light. *That's not right.* She flipped on the light and looked around at her mother's spotless kitchen, then made her way to the sink to wash her plate and wipe down the table.

Half past midnight, she sat in her window seat thinking. Love, shift, and forgiveness. These themes rolled over and over in her mind. She loved her parents, but there needed to be some shift in those relationships. But what about the facts? As an attorney she was trained to examine and deal with the facts. But it wasn't facts that had led her to the place where she was wrong. It was love.

She loved her mother and should forgive her for appearing to be so weak and ineffectual. She needed to seek her mother's forgiveness for all the wrongs she'd covered up for her father. And she would also ask her sisters to forgive her. Yvette, for not helping out more with Quanny. And Dena for being a poor big sister, and especially for not telling Dena that Daddy had a PI investigating her. She'd have to ask her sisters to forgive her for being such a judgmental bitch.

But Daddy, he was a different subject. She couldn't forgive him. Not for the position he'd placed her in. She hung her head in guilt for the things she'd done to protect her father. *Are you ready to forgive yourself?* Kitty paced her room. It had been a long time since that still, small voice within her had spoken. She shook her head, not ready to deal with herself. She shifted the focus of her attention.

"What about Davis?" she whispered. She had one question for him. She glanced at her clock and saw it was close to 1 a.m. But she needed to know, so she picked up the phone.

"Hey." His voice was husky.

She sucked in her lower lip. She was a selfish little girl for waking him up. "I'm sorry, I shouldn't have awakened you."

He cleared his throat. "I wasn't asleep."

"Don't lie."

"Now woman, I've told you twice. I don't lie. Really, I wasn't asleep. I was lying here thinking of you."

"Oh, really? What were you thinking?"

She heard the rustle of the bed clothes as he shifted position. "How it hurts my back when I have to bend over to kiss you."

"And…"

He inhaled. "And about that thing you did the other night with your breast."

"No." She drew her lip in between her front teeth. Sex was not what she needed to discuss. "Okay, that's not why I called."

"You asked, and I've got to tell you the truth. What's on your mind, counselor?"

"Davis, I can't forget what you said to me on Saturday night."

"What are you saying?"

There was tension and maybe a hint of fear in his voice.

"Help me through this, Davis. I want to forgive you, but I don't know how. I don't want to forget your words because they were all true and I want to grow from them. And I want us to stay together, but I think we need to slow down, like Mama Cat says." She sat down on her bed. "How do we get through this?"

"Hold on, Kitty. I want to turn on the light."

Chapter 15

Davis glanced over the paper copy of his daily agenda. All tasks, all to-do boxes checked off, except one. One more meeting. He studied the page and nodded his approval. Despite her ghetto-fabulous appearance, Glynnis did a good job as his administrator. His days were laid out exactly as he'd asked, everything scheduled with half-hour intervals in between so he was always on time.

He thought about what wasn't inked in on his calendar page. Today was a big day for Kitty. He checked the clock on his computer; she should be just about to end the settlement meeting between her father and his son.

"Lord, let it go well for her, for the family. No, Lord, for all concerned. Amen."

The knock of his last appointment stirred him from his prayer. He rose and walked over to answer.

"Hi, Terri Taylor, come on in." He cocked his head to the side as she entered. Terri sauntered in slowly. For full effect? Her V-necked red dress of a clingy material hugged her ample curves. Principals never dressed like this when he was in school.

Phat Head lurched.

Terri turned and smiled. "Hi, Davis, thanks for seeing me."

"Sorry it had to be so late." Since Glynnis had left early to get her hair done, he pushed the door back and left it standing wide open.

Terry moved toward the sofa. "No, this is great. It gave me a chance to go home and get cleaned up."

Cleaned up. Her hair bounced with fresh curls. He hadn't really noticed before, but made up she had a pretty face. His eyes slipped down to her wide hips.

His neck snapped as he lifted his gaze. "Err, why don't you sit over here." He motioned to the wingback chairs in front of his desk and strode over to settle in behind that barrier. "What can I do for you?"

Terry gushed and prattled on for several minutes about how glad everyone was that he'd moved home. "Your uncles are already talking about you taking your father's seat on the deacon board."

He smiled. "More like campaigning for it." Those old goats had already made an appointment for him to speak to the pastor.

She continued the compliments for the next five minutes, everything from his speech at the Christmas party to his selection of neighborhood, same as hers. He glanced at his watch. It was almost time to talk to Kitty. His stomach growled. "Thank you, Terri. Why did you want to see me?"

She pulled at the edge of her dress and wiggled a bit in the chair. "I'm the general chair for this year's church anniversary, and since it's our fiftieth year I think we should do something special, like a dinner dance. That way we can celebrate and also raise funds for the scholarships."

He nodded. "And you want to have it here at the Center? That's simple. Just call Glynnis and schedule a date."

"Yes, thank you. But there was something more." She reached up and pulled at a strand of her hair.

"Oh, yeah, of course. We'll only charge the church for the cost of the meals."

She grimaced. "I'd really appreciate that...."

He lowered his head. "But you want something more?"

"Yes. I was hoping that we could also do something to honor the Rock Hill Nine, given the role our church played in that history."

He nodded. Their church had been a guiding light in the civil rights activities of Rock Hill. The Rock Hill Nine had held some of its organizing meetings in their old building. The church was very proud of that heritage. The elders made sure all the children were infused with that knowledge. It was those teachings that had inspired him into a life of service. But according to Lou, in recent years those teachings had faded.

"Our civil rights pioneers are getting up in age, and I think now's the time to honor them. Maybe we can ask our congressman to come and present some kind of citation. That would really bring out the town dignitaries and even statewide politicians. We could sell a lot of tickets."

"Sure, I think that's all great. But let me talk to Kitty before you send out any invitations. Mr. Franklin seems to have a sensitivity about his ties to the Nine."

Her smile faded. Terri sighed and babbled on about her other plans for the church anniversary gala.

Davis picked up a pen and checked off the last box. Closer to talking to his baby, he stood. "That all sounds fine. Just keep me posted on the plans and let me know what I need to do to help."

"Thanks, Davis." She gathered her bag.

He glanced out of the window. The gray day had dissolved into night. "If you can wait a minute, I'll walk you to your car. It's getting dark out, and there's only a small investment club meeting tonight at the center. There aren't many people around, and Penny's most likely gone home for dinner." He collected his briefcase and escorted her out of the building.

As they walked across the lot and neared her Lexus, his phone rang.

"How'd it go, baby?" he answered. "Yes, I'm just finishing up. I'm walking Terri to her car. Can I call you back in a minute?"

"Terri from Texas?"

Her demanding screech echoed in his ear. The last thing he wanted was to get her ire up again.

"Yeah."

"Is she standing there? Does she know you're talking to me? Did she hear you call me baby?" Kitty snapped.

"Yes, baby. I love you, Miss Catherine Franklin," he said, louder than necessary. "I'll call you back in a minute."

"You better, and in less than a minute."

Davis grinned and put his phone in his pocket. How'd he fall in love with such a rude woman? He turned toward the crestfallen Terri. "Sorry about that."

She shrugged. "Can I ask you a question?"

"Sure."

Terri examined the asphalt and her shoes. "Your mother tells me you two haven't been together long. How do you keep a long-distance relationship working?"

His smile widened. Just the other day, Sharon had shared with him how Terri's last relationship, a long distance Internet affair, had failed. "We have dinner together every night. Well, I have dinner. Kitty usually eats something out of a white box."

Terri looked up. Her disappointment softened in the yellow glow of the street light. "How?"

"Technology. Webcams." He opened her car door and waited for her to settle behind the wheel before saying good night. Thirty seconds left for him to get to his car and call his girl. Kitty was so cute when she let her insecurities show. He'd come to know that her bark was just that, barking.

She wasn't available when he called. The only time she didn't pick up his calls was when she had her father on the line. For her sake he prayed that Roosevelt had settled his business today. He hoped that God had answered his prayers and had given Kitty a measure of grace for today. As traumatic as this experience had been for her, his heart went out to the boy. Another young black man who grew up without his father in the home. Knowing that his father was a powerful congressman had to affect him. He prayed mightily for the son.

He drove out to his mother's house. Lou's newfound pleasure was to keep a hot plate ready for her son. He set up his laptop computer and Internet wireless card so he could video chat with his sweetheart. For them the nightly webcam dates were the next best thing to being there. He was on his second helping of baked chicken before Kitty called. He clicked the answer icon on his laptop. When her picture came up on the screen, he frowned.

"Kitty, this is the fourth night in a row you've eaten out of a Styrofoam box. You need to come on home and get a proper meal." He wanted her to share the warmth of his mother's kitchen. His webcam was not the best, but he could make out the scowl that crossed her face.

"I'll go home tomorrow and see what my mother cooks. Dena's going with me. Daddy's getting plump, and she's been here less than a week. That always happens when she's in DC. But I think she's leaving soon." She dug her fork into her Chinese takeout box. "What are you eating? I see you're in your mother's kitchen again. Getting plump?"

"Mama's real happy to have somebody to cook and care for."

She twisted her neck and waved her finger at the camera. "Then she needs to find herself a man and stop trying to fatten mine up again."

Davis laughed so hard he kicked the table and upset the connection. While he restored his link he sent a text message.

ROFL, ROLLING ON THE FLOOR LAUGHING.

In spite of her delivery, Kitty was right. He was her man and his mother was trying to put some more meat on his bones. His router took forever to reset. Service was sometimes spotty in the back woods of Rock Hill. He picked up his BlackBerry to call. He turned over the words in his head while it rang. What was the best way to ask Kitty to leave her father and come home to take care of her man? They'd had long conversations about life and the mysteries of marriage over the past few days. He'd told her about his parents' commitment. They married, raised a family, and had been faithful unto death. And after. Lou still refused to accept any gentlemen callers.

The Franklin marriage was very different. Kitty described it as a never-ending circle. Roosevelt would commit the unpardonable sin, Yesenia would forgive him. And then it would happen again. But that was all from Kitty's point of view since, as she explained, Yesenia never discussed the intimate details of her marriage with anyone. It was a family mantra: a relationship is between two people.

He wondered if Kitty had extended this teaching to their relationship. Had she told anyone what had happened between them? No, he was confident that neither of her sisters knew her business, although she knew all of theirs.

Thanks to her father's team of investigators, Kitty knew everything her sisters were up to. He knew Kitty hated her mother's advice, but he was nothing but grateful for it. Because of Yesenia's teaching he wouldn't be embarrassed to go around her family again.

At last the reward of the connection: Kitty's smile on screen and a sweet text on his BlackBerry.

I LOVE YOU BUT I CAN'T COOK.

"Come home, Kitty."

"Dave, we've been over that. I can't this weekend. It's the congressional Christmas party and I can't miss the look on my father's face when Dena walks in with her boyfriend."

As if the Franklins didn't have enough on their plates. Kitty's PI had taken pictures of Dena having sex in several public spaces with the son of a Jewish congressman from California. Her parents were furious, and Dena was afraid to bring him to the house. It was decided the safest place for the families to meet would be at the congressional Christmas party.

"Baby, I mean come home to stay."

"Stop, Davis. I thought we went through this last night. I'm just not sure I'm ready. There are so many things I still have to do before I could even consider leaving Daddy. And today we got word of another problem." Her voice shook. "A congressional ethics investigation."

He stared at the ceiling and wondered if he was wasting his time. Was there no end to Roosevelt Franklin's troubles? Would Kitty ever be strong enough to leave her father and cleave only unto him?

"Baby, I really admire you for the way you honor and respect your parents, but isn't it time for you to live your own life?"

There was silence on the line.

"Davis, I hear you, but I also saw your contract. You can't afford me." She gave a nervous chuckle.

And that mouth. He'd decided to accept that, but would he ever get used to it? Since he wanted to spend his evening with her, he let her get away with changing the subject. He did the same and broached the questions that had been in the back of his mind since his meeting with Terri. "Kitty, why doesn't your father like to speak about the Rock Hill Nine?"

"Because it was supposed to be the Rock Hill Ten. Daddy ducked out on his boys. And some of them have never forgiven him."

"I know that much. Uncle Charlie tells me that they were a right tight band of brothers. But why would they hold a grudge for something like that? I mean, I respect how hard it was for them to spend time in jail, but it all turned out for the better for our community. And your father's done a lot of good work in this district. Why was he a no-show anyway? I never got that part of the story."

Kitty tossed her head and leaned back into her chair. "What have you heard?"

"I heard that he was at Friendship College at the time, and your grandmother was working three jobs to pay his tuition. And that she left the church because she was fourscore against him participating in any kind of protest. I can understand how she didn't want him to get into any trouble. But is she really still holding a grudge against the church for holding the organizing meetings?"

"Yeah, Mama Cat doesn't back down. To this day she still refuses to step foot in any Baptist Methodist Assembly church. She wants to hear you sing, though, so you've got her close to relenting. She really likes you. But that's not it." Kitty careened her neck around as if she were looking into his mother's kitchen. "There's no one else around, is there?" She waited for his confirmation. "If you want, I'll tell you a family secret."

Davis moved closer to the small eye at the top of his laptop.

Kitty moved back from the camera on her side. "Daddy missed the meeting because he was with my mother."

"What's so secret about that?"

"At that time she was somebody else's girl." Kitty shook her head.

"I see."

"He'll never change. But obviously my mother knows this firsthand. He tries to stay away from the story lest those who were there remember. Why do you ask?"

He told her about his meeting with Terri and her request.

"The church should send a letter to his office and copy me. I'll make sure he issues some congressional proclamation honoring the church's role in the protest. But don't count on him coming. He might send my mother."

"Dave, you still here?" The screen door slammed behind Lou as she entered the house from the back porch. "Is the princess still talking to you on that computer?" Lovenia walked over to the screen and put her face squarely in front of the webcam. "Hey, Princess." She moved back from the screen so she could see Kitty.

"Turn around so I can see it better. Girl, I like that more every day," Lou said. Kitty turned around so she could see her full head. "You look just like a little pixie fairy." She clapped her hands and approved again of Kitty's haircut.

"How's your family, baby? And you aren't having anymore of those sick headaches, are you? And when you coming back home?" Lou bombarded her with the usual questions.

Davis tried to stop her. "Come on, Mom." Lou cut her eyes at him. Kitty and Lou had their fifteen minutes of conversation every time he was here. He picked up his plate to wash it. He was glad they were developing their own relationship. Kitty's respectful treatment of his mother revealed a lot about her character.

"Princess, I can't wait to hear how it all turns out this weekend with Dena."

"Me, either, but wait for me to give you the lowdown personally. I'm sure some lies or half truths will come out all over the blogs before the salad is served on Saturday night."

"Now you know Davis has banned us all from the blogs and chat rooms." Both women laughed.

Davis wiped down the kitchen counters. "When will you two be through gossiping?" He stood behind Lou. "Okay, Mama, can I get the screen back?"

Lou turned her head slowly to regard her son. "No." She turned back to Kitty. "Princess, you let my boy go now, so he can get home and get to bed. He can call you again once he gets home. But don't call him in the car. I don't want him talking on the phone and driving. That's dangerous and it gets dark back up in these woods," Lou fussed. Davis just laughed.

Later than night Davis was back on the phone with Kitty. He'd been working at his desk when he opened his mail and found another one of the loving notes she often mailed him. He picked up the phone.

"Come on home, Kitty," he started in as soon as she answered.

"Davis, it's late. You should be in bed."

"I just read your letter. Thank you, lady. I love you, too, and I want you to come home. And if you don't feel comfortable staying with me, stay at your mother's house. I want to court you properly, like Mama Cat says."

"Davis, we've already discussed—"

"Don't interrupt me, woman. I was just thinking how nice it could be if I could come sit with you on the porch while your grandmother chaperones. I want to take you to the show, and on Friday nights around here we all go to the high school game. Whatever they're playing, football or basketball. You do realize that we've never gone to a concert or taken a moonlight stroll? I want to do all these things with you."

"Sounds like you want to date me on the cheap," she teased.

He continued, "I want to take you to Chicago. I want you to meet my friends, the Gates."

"Oh, free dinner at somebody's house?'

"No, smarty. And when you meet Finus Gates you'll know that nothing around him is ever cheap. Let me take you shopping on the magnificent mile."

"Oh, goody. When can we go?"

"Not until spring. It's too cold for you this time of year." He chuckled. "No, I take it back. I see you strolling down Michigan Avenue wrapped in fur."

"I'd like that, but I don't own a fur coat. Daddy gets more mileage out of the PETA people than the fur lobby."

He paused, a bit put off again that her daddy played such a prominent role in her life. He believed in honoring one's parents, but this was ridiculous. "All the ladies I know in the Windy City wear fur. So you'll need a fur, too. Wait a minute, I'm trying to picture it now. What color would you like, white or dark?"

"What about a foxy brown?"

Silence sat between them while he pondered a stray thought. "Lord, what am I going to do? Girl, I was just trying to figure out how many speeches I'd have to give to buy you a fur."

"Davis, you don't have to spoil me like that."

A huge grin covered his face. "You really are growing. And I'm so proud. And I am going to spoil you, although I should know better."

"Oh, no, you're not going to work yourself into a grave trying to buy me things. Davis, I've got a job and I'll be content to go to a high school football game or moonlit walk just to be with you."

"I love that sweet, sassy mouth of yours." He turned out the lights in his den and headed toward his bedroom. They stayed up late into the night discussing his finances and how they might live on his salary. It wouldn't be easy, but if they both made concessions it could work. Davis glanced over at the clock; twelve forty-five. "Kitty, let's try. Come home for Christmas. Let's see if we can survive two weeks together."

"No, I want to go to the Cayman Islands for the holidays." She sounded almost as if she were pouting. "I need some sunshine and clear blue water to clear my head. I'd like to bring in the New Year with sand and room service."

"Girl, I just bought a house. I don't think I can swing that."

"There's a place I know where you can check in under an assumed name and pay cash. And you don't have to worry about a dime. Daddy's going to give you a Christmas bonus. He's happy with your work. I think it's going to be a lot of money. We can use it for the trip."

"Uh, I don't know what all that means, but I just got back here to Rock Hill so you need to know I'm not going anywhere. They've got me singing in a Christmas cantata at church and Jackie'll be here the day after Christmas. But it's beyond just Christmas. You need to accept the fact that I'm not inclined to leave here anytime soon."

"Come on, Davis."

"Not this Christmas, Kitty. But beyond the holidays, you know what we're talking about. Can you commit to living in Rock Hill and on my salary?"

Kitty exhaled loudly.

He impatiently waited for her response by flipping through the rest of his mail. Mostly sales circulars from the local department stores.

"I'm so sick of Washington politics, I don't know what to do. I've lived in Rock Hill before. As long as I can get to the airport I'm good."

"Now, girl, I don't make the kind of money that will see you traveling 'round the world."

"I know what you make, and Davis, I can do a lot from home and I have Twanna. But I'll have to make frequent trips to the District to do my job. Are you willing to accept that?"

"To start."

"And since you won't budge out of Rock Hill this year, I'll come home for Christmas."

"Great."

After they hung up he sat up in bed for a while. He felt happy and sad. Their unconventional relationship would work better if she weren't so connected to her father.

Chapter 16

Kitty picked up her BlackBerry and scrolled through her messages. Two from Davis, but she dared not call him back. On Sunday afternoon the prospective Deacon Davis Thornton was probably still in church. She shoved the phone back into her pocket. She should have gone home this weekend just to be with him. Despite the fireworks from her father, the congressional Christmas party last night had been boring without Davis. Even if it meant sitting in church all day, she should have gone home to be with him and sit on her mother's porch with him as he'd asked.

Anything would beat being stuck in this session with a team of lawyers and political strategists. Twenty years ago this would have been the proverbial smoked-filled room. But today it was littered with empty water bottles and the remains of a sandwich tray. Kitty peered out the window. For all of his seniority her father only had a view of the Longworth House office building. The off-white stone was most likely cold today. She rubbed her hands together; they were cold, too. Lately everything in DC seemed cold and unfriendly.

"Kitty, if you need a break I think we could all use one."

She focused her attention on Tom Ridgel, the senior member of today's team.

"Yeah, sure."

Everyone sighed and stood to stretch or check their personal communication devices. Tom moved over to the sideboard, probably to make another sandwich. Over the years he'd grown rotund and grandfatherly. He was definitely the person to handle the latest. Her father had put Tom in front of this because of Tom's connections and credentials. Her father and three of his Congressional Black Caucus cronies were being investigated by the house ethics committee about the foundation's scholarship fund. The team of lawyers, his male chief of staff, and new professional media consultant had spent the bulk of the day trying to construct a positive spin for this one.

Tom picked at the remains of the sandwich tray and motioned her over. "How are you doing with all of this?"

"What's that supposed to mean?" she snapped and cut her eyes at him. Whenever there was a break in the action Tom treated her like Roosevelt's daughter, not a fellow attorney.

"Come on, Tiger. You look a little tired."

Bless his conservative republican heart. He was the only one allowed to call her Tiger. Tom had been with them for so long he was like a caring uncle. She smiled. "I'm fine."

Tom waddled over and wrapped a flabby arm around her shoulder. "Stop trying to bullshit the old shitter. I don't know how you handle this. He's your father, and some of the things he told us today…" Tom shook his head.

"At this point nothing surprises me." Kitty looked down at her boots. Before he left earlier this afternoon Daddy had unloaded a boatload. The common people just couldn't catch a break. Even something good like a scholarship fund got clouded inside the beltway. The initial investigation questioned whether CBC scholarships were being traded for favors and rewards, and, in more than one case, just blatantly given out to relatives. But with all the corporate donations and suspect record keeping, new questions were surfacing about where all the cash was really going.

"I've got this, you know. It's actually simple if we can stay on top of the press spin. This place is run on corporate cash; nobody wants to open that can. I've got some visits scheduled for tomorrow. We should have this cleaned up by Wednesday." Tom reached into his pocket for a packet of gum. Gum was his new bad habit since no one really smoked anymore. Tom had the best connections on Capitol Hill. He also knew where more than a few bodies were buried. A few well-placed visits from him might just stop the investigation. "I've seen this one before."

She laughed. Tom often joked that the black lawmakers weren't doing anything the white legislators hadn't already done. The only difference was that the black lawmakers had come late too the party. Her father had snapped Tom up as soon as Chicago's Dan Rostenkowski left office.

"We know and we trust you."

"Good. Now you go home. I hear your mother's cooking. I'll call you if we need anything." Tom reached for a cup to spit out the gum. He couldn't stand chewing gum. "I'll walk you out, Tiger, and after this, it's the Chinese Wall."

"After today's disclosures that would be best." Staying away from this would allow her to better protect her father's interests if Tom was unsuccessful, and it would give her more time to follow up with her own investigations. Tee still hadn't found out who owned the blog dedicated to embarrassing her father. "Guess I'm leaving. My mother has planned one of her old-fashioned Sunday dinners and I'm already going to be late for the fireworks." Kitty gathered her papers, removing a few. Now that the Chinese Wall was up, there were some documents best not in her possession.

"I'm surprised she's feeding Rosey today. I heard she was pretty angry at the way he acted at the party last night."

She closed her bag. "Walk with me."

This was the way it worked. DC was a beast that feasted on gossip, and Tom was a primary chef.

"Tell them we're starting again in five," Tom said to the receptionist as they walked past.

Kitty waved at the young girl still in her church clothes. The new receptionist was a plain, ultra-religious church girl Yesenia had insisted she hire.

As they walked through the empty halls of the Rayburn Office Building she gave Tom a few morsels for his meetings tomorrow.

"You know Dena's dating Congressman Stein's son. And that Daddy showed his tail a bit last night."

Tom's face glowed. "You're sounding awful Southern lately."

She glanced over at Tom and decided to sidestep his comment. "He stepped outside with Congressman Stein last night and had a few angry words."

"About the pictures?"

"Damn, is nothing secret in this town?" Kitty shook her head. "We paid a pretty penny for that camera chip. It would kill my mother if those ever hit the street."

"Okay, that's enough for me. You know a lot of people really like Yesenia, so I think that will quell interest in seeking those photos. Now that this is out, we'll have our share of pictures of Dena and Levi out in public. It'll be enough for the Hill tomorrow that Roosevelt Franklin's daughter is in an interracial relationship. And I've met with Stein. The outside extracurricular activities will stop." Tom's eyes twinkled. "Now just one more thing, Tiger."

They stopped at the security checkpoint.

"How's your love life?"

Kitty reached up and hugged Tom. "None of your business, but thanks for asking."

She hurried past the checkpoint and hopped into her car. "Call Davis," she commanded her phone as soon as she turned onto Independence Avenue. When the call wasn't answered, she left a message. "Guess there was no reason for me to come home since you're still in church. Call me when you can."

After turning the radio from talk to some contemporary R&B, she headed across the Potomac to her parents' house. In five minutes she switched back to talk. Somehow the lines between R&B and contemporary gospel had been blurred. It was hard for her to listen to songs of praise and salvation when every day she felt more lost.

Dealing with her father's constant political and personal problems was like bailing water from a leaky boat in the midst of a storm. Just when it seemed that the seas were calm, another squall erupted. For a few minutes Kitty focused on the news and the teaser given by the talk show host for the upcoming topic "What's wrong with the black man in America?" While it was sure to be a lively discussion, it wasn't something she wanted to hear, so she switched back to the R&B station.

There wasn't much wrong with her man. He shared some of her father's good qualities but overall Davis was nothing like her father. Things were going well for her and Davis. "Over phone and video chat," she confided in her dashboard. They hadn't found the opportunity to actually be together. But that hadn't stopped them from growing closer, she thought.

After she'd decided to forgive him, the relationship seemed to deepen. Davis had just said that distance/absence was making his heart grow fonder. He was everything she never knew she wanted. Honest, kind, patient, loving.

"Tall, dark, handsome and sexy." She grinned. "Thank you, Jesus," she screamed out. "Thank you, Lord," she sang along with a contemporary Christian song from the radio. As the song ended she turned onto her parents' street. She shook her head. She'd have to tell Lou and Davis about the little praise party she'd just had in the car. Lou would be proud and Davis would ask if she were shifting.

There was one car too many in the driveway. She grimaced. This meant company for dinner. She really was too tired to sit through dinner with anyone except her immediate family. If she weren't trying to be a better daughter to her mother, she'd pull out of the drive and go home.

Kitty took a deep breath as she entered the house. She really wasn't in the mood to put on a Franklin family friendly smile for company. Not after her day. Her father's Sunday confessions really weighted on her. All she wanted to do was eat, talk to Dena, play with Quanny for a bit, then go home and spend the night with Davis. On the phone.

Yesenia attacked her before she could close the door. "Kitty, it's about time."

She stood back on her heels.

"Now hurry upstairs and put on a dress and some makeup," her mother said.

"Aw, Mom, come on," she said as anger flashed in her eyes. She checked over her mother's outfit. Full dress for a Sunday afternoon dinner: St. John skirt suit, pumps, and pearls. "Who's your dinner guest?"

"Somebody special, and we've already waited too long for you. Go get dressed and stop by your father's study before you come to the dining room." Her mother stepped back and winked at her.

Her mother was so ridiculous, she smiled.

" 'Senia, is that Kitty?" Roosevelt called out.

"Hurry," her mother whispered before hurrying off in the direction of the study.

Since she was hungry and the house smelled like home cooking, she complied with her mother's request. *The sooner we eat. The sooner I'm out of here.*

Ten minutes later, freshly pressed and hopefully up to her mother's standards, Kitty opened the door to her father's study.

"Oh, my God, Davis," she squealed and ran into his open arms.

"My pretty Kitty," he purred in her ear as he kissed her.

She held onto him tightly. "How, when, why didn't you tell me?"

His mustache quivered against her cheek. "Surprise."

"This is a blessing," she blurted out. "I thought you'd be in church all day."

"Yeah." He pulled away for just a second. "You look so pretty."

She pulled him close and kissed him again. "Let's sit before your back starts to hurt."

"No, ma'am, I think we better get into that dining room before I get into trouble with your mother. We've got the rest of today and all night to sit together."

She took his hand and two steps toward the door. "Wait, you're missing evening service and probably some of the morning worship." Davis still had to pass a vote to assume his father's seat on the deacon board. "That's not going to bode well for you with the rest of the board."

"No, baby, I'm not. Thank you for asking. Pastor Janelle went into labor last night so all we did was pray and give praise for her healthy baby boy and Uncle Ralph dismissed us. I hopped on the first thing smoking. And the Center's now closed on Mondays."

One of Davis's first decisions had been to close the administrative offices on Monday since the staff worked most weekends. They walked hand-in-hand to the dining room. She stopped just before entering.

"Hey," she whispered and tugged on his hand. He leaned down. "Sorry in advance for what's about to happen."

"Kitty, I've been here several hours already. I've already been through the grilling." He smiled.

"Get in here, I'm ready to eat," Roosevelt's voice boomed over them.

"Davis, you come sit next to me and Kitty, over there next to your father," Yesenia directed. In classic Yesenia Franklin fashion, dinner was formal and she had arranged a seating chart: father at the head of the table, mother at the opposite end, Kitty next to her father, as always. Her shoulders slumped. She couldn't be that far away from Davis, not even for her mother's cooking.

"No. Dena, will you please come sit next to Daddy and let me sit by Davis?" She cast a pleading look at her younger sister.

"Uhhh," Dena shook her head no.

"Then sit next to Quanny; I'll sit by Daddy." Yvette rose from her seat, which was usually as far away from their father as she could get.

"Enough of these musical chairs. Everybody sit down somewhere so I can eat," Roosevelt yelled. With that the girls all found new seats and dinner was served.

"How come you didn't tell me?" Kitty sat on Davis's lap in her mother's parlor hours later. After dinner she'd had to give him up so he could spend time with her father. It seemed that they were in his study man talking for hours. Then that was followed by the 'let's take Davis to see the national Christmas tree and holiday lights' trip. She had patiently endured a cold DC evening because of his enthusiasm for seeing the sights.

"I tried to get you all afternoon. I finally called here and your mother told me where you were and to come straight here. And I don't care what you say about your mother, she is interested in what's going on in our relationship."

Kitty furrowed her brow. "I know she didn't ask you anything about us."

"Not directly." He kissed the top of her nose. "But she sat and attentively listened while your sisters asked all the questions. Yvette and Dena are just as nosy as my mom."

"What did you tell them?"

"Nothing, none of their business. Judging from their questions, you haven't told them anything, either. Still trying to keep me as your closet boo." He grinned.

"Hey, we've been taught that if you want your family to respect your man, you don't tell them anything about said man. And I want them to respect you because you are…" she kissed him slowly, "you are worthy."

"Thank you." He squeezed her tightly, then lifted her gently off his lap. She stood up. "Let's go home."

"No, ma'am. I'm spending the night right here. I wanted to check into a hotel but your mother wouldn't hear of it. I'm here to court you properly, so I think I'm sleeping on the sofa in your father's study."

Kitty sat back down and poked her lip out. "Then I'm staying, too, and as soon as my folks are asleep—"

"No, ma'am, not in your parents' house."

Kitty pressed her chest against his and licked his lips.

"Don't get me in trouble with your mother, 'cause I'm already on thin ice with your father."

"I know he's pleased with how you're running the Center."

"He's not pleased about us."

Kitty hopped up and yelled, "Daddy!"

Davis grabbed for her hand. "Stop that, Kitty. I can handle my problems with your father."

She rushed to the door to stop her father. "Never mind," she said as soon as Roosevelt appeared in the hall.

Chapter 17

"Kitty, Kitty." Dena cracked open the door to their father's study. "Kitty, are you up?"

"Umm, Dena." Kitty sat up and stretched. The sofa bed in the study wasn't the softest place to sleep.

"I wanted to make sure you got out of here before Daddy gets up," Dena said from the doorway.

"It's okay, Dena, come in. Davis isn't in here. He slept upstairs in my room. This sofa wasn't big enough for him."

Dena sauntered into the room and draped herself over one of the leather wingback chairs. "Oh, so he needs a king-sized bed to do little ole you?"

Kitty laughed. Dena was a lot like Twanna. She was so glad their relationship had recently benefited from a healthy dose of forgiveness. "No, 'cause as you know, things can be done in a very small space."

"Oh, that's a good one," Dena hooted without any resentment or anger.

Kitty swung her feet onto the floor. "I couldn't let Davis sleep on this bumpy old thing."

Dena looked closely at her for a moment. "You love him."

Kitty blushed and nodded.

"Wait here." Dena jumped up and ran toward the door.

"Where are you going?"

"To get the camera and Yvette. We've got to document this moment. Kitty's in love."

Kitty stretched and yawned. She was tired. They hadn't gotten much sleep last night; Davis had insisted that they behave in her parent's house, despite her willingness to do more. And that was one more thing that she loved about him. He was respectful.

And because of him, she and her sisters were getting along, a positive shift. It was Davis who had encouraged her to seek their forgiveness. From Dena forgiveness came quickly. She'd been softened by her boyfriend Levi's free spirit. Dena had adopted his Zen philosophy; the California guy held no grudges and kept no records. Kitty could see how much Zen had helped with Dena's relationship with their father.

Yvette was trying to forgive and shift but was slow. She still held onto a lot of anger. And somehow she'd shifted the bulk of her anger about Reggie's upcoming wedding to their father. Kitty made a mental note to spend some time with Yvette and Quanny in the upcoming week. Her sister needed more support.

After Dena came back with the camera, the sisters sat on the pull-out sofa bed giggling and teasing Kitty.

"It's been too long since we've laughed like this," Dena said. She'd always been the most easygoing of the sisters.

It felt good to hang out with her sisters without fighting. "I'm so glad we were all home for Sunday dinner and you two got to spend some time with Davis," Kitty said.

"He's cool," Dena said approvingly.

Yvette nodded. "Mom's up, I can smell the coffee." She stood and stretched. "I can use a cup and some biscuits. I hope she's baking this morning."

Dena also stood and stretched her long frame. "I think I'll go help her."

Kitty smiled, another side effect of forgiveness and shift. They'd all decided to help their mother out a little more when she was in town. "I'll get up and come, too."

"Oh, no, you stay here." Dena held up her hands and stopped at the door. "I want to hear Daddy yelling when he knocks on this door and you answer."

Kitty laughed and got out of bed. Before she left Davis upstairs in her room she'd put a few things in a clothes basket. She got dressed and waited for her father. If she knew him, it wouldn't be long before he knocked.

Dena had awakened Davis earlier in her quest to keep Kitty out of their father's crosshairs. Since he wanted to be a good houseguest he got up and dressed. He was at the top of the stairs when he heard the congressman bellow.

"No, Kitty. Not in my house. Yesenia, Yesenia," Roosevelt howled.

He hurried toward the study just in time to see the Franklin women totally convulsed in laughter. Dena was doubled over, and Mrs. Franklin had lifted her apron to cover the mirth on her face.

"Okay, that's enough. You all have had your laugh." Roosevelt Franklin drew himself up and tried to bring order to his women. "Dena, I know you set this up." The lion of the Congressional Black Caucus tried again to restore order.

Davis wasn't sure what was going on, so he stood back and watched.

"What's so funny, Mama? I don't get it," Quanny said.

"Get my baby out of here," Roosevelt yelled at Yvette and stomped into his room. "And you, turn off that TV and get out of my study," he yelled at Kitty.

A moment later Kitty left the study and the door slammed behind her.

"Good morning, Davis." Kitty practically pounced on him as the others turned toward the kitchen.

"What's going on? What did Dena do to your father?"

Kitty held onto his arm as another fit of laughter overtook her. When she composed herself she explained the practical joke.

"Dena ordered a porn movie from the cable service and turned it up loud. So when Daddy…" She took a deep breath. "Whoo. So when Daddy came down and stood by this door he heard, he thought he heard…"

Davis put up his hand. "That's enough, I get it. Now y'all know that was wrong."

"Yeah, but so worth it. Daddy was so mad I think he turned blue." She took another deep breath. "It's okay, he'll get over it real soon. Come on, let's get some breakfast. My mother made her famous biscuits and he's not going to let anything keep him from missing honey and heaven." She pulled his arm. "A fresh batch should be coming out of the oven any minute now. My mother makes her biscuits in small batches so everyone can get them piping hot."

Davis hesitated. Dena didn't realize what her joke might cost him. Roosevelt Franklin had made himself very clear last night when they spoke in his study. He was grateful that Roosevelt hadn't seen him standing in the hallway. The man might have shot him just for the picture he had formed in his head from Dena's joke.

"So what are you guys doing today?" Dena asked while Davis devoured his second batch of biscuits.

He chewed. His mother made good biscuits, but Yesenia Franklin's were heavenly light. "Umm," he said, chewing. "I thought maybe Kitty would take me sightseeing. Then I want to take her to the mall to do some Christmas shopping." He wiped his hand on a napkin and pushed away from the table.

"The mall," Yvette scoffed. "You don't really know Kitty that well, do you? Kitty doesn't shop at malls."

He glanced over at Kitty, who nodded in confirmation.

Dena rose and walked with her empty plate to the sink. "I hope Daddy's paying you a fortune because little Kitty likes the little boutique shops, where they sell little high-heeled shoes." She rubbed her ring finger and thumb together to indicate how much little shoes could cost.

"Whatever she wants," he said. "I better not have another bite," he complimented Yesenia. "How have I been so blessed to have breakfast with four, no, five, beautiful women?" He winked at Quanny. All three generations of the Franklin women gushed. Roosevelt would surely have some comment if he'd seen this. Roosevelt was so angry about Dena's joke that he hadn't joined them for breakfast. He'd had his wife bring his plate to him in the study.

The sightseeing trip Davis planned was delayed. Before they could leave the house Kitty had to field a phone call. An investigative reporter from the Washington Post was looking for an angle on the congressional ethics probe involving the Congressional Black Caucus scholarship fund. Somebody had given the reporter a tidbit about the son of a woman who worked at the State Department, a woman who'd once worked for Congressman Franklin, whose son had just been awarded a full ride scholarship at Georgetown.

Davis watched Kitty closely as she attempted to dispatch the reporter with some prepared answers. She seemed to be able to detach herself from the fact that the reporter was asking about her father's son. To ensure that the matter was settled and the reporter would let the angle die, she immediately phoned an attorney she called Uncle Tom.

Davis sat for a while in the office with Roosevelt and Kitty as they dealt with the aftermath of the reporter's unanswered questions. Davis and Kitty left the house at midday and tried to enjoy the afternoon. But Kitty's phone was a constant interruption. If it wasn't Twanna calling, it was Uncle Tom.

"That reporter kept digging and I think he's found something," she said while they shopped in her favorite stationary store. He knew most of the cards she picked out were for him, so he cheerfully paid for them.

"I've got to call Daddy," she said while they waited for a sales clerk to bring the shoes she'd selected at her favorite shoe boutique. Dena was right, Kitty's little shoes were expensive. He'd have to take on some speaking engagements to buy the red Italian leather boots she was eyeing.

Kitty protested when he offered to buy her the three pairs of shoes she'd tried on. But then her phone rang and she decided not to buy anything.

Davis left her in a quiet corner in the back of a coffee shop and wandered about DuPont Circle on his own. He frowned. He'd hoped to get a good idea of what she liked so his Christmas presents would please her. But she couldn't disengage long enough to spend a simple afternoon Christmas shopping with him. As he walked he couldn't help feeling doubts about the relationship. And how could she cover up for so much wrong? The way she detached herself from the truth was discouraging.

He circled the fountain at DuPont Circle twice before Kitty called. She didn't have good news. She asked him to meet her by the pylon marker for the metro train; they had to get back to the house.

"The reporter from the Post came to the door. He wanted to interview my mother," she told him as they descended into the DuPont Circle metro station. "She is very upset." She took another call and hand motioned him through the station to hop on the train. "What aggravates me most is that I think the guy knew all along what the real story was. He was just baiting me and Daddy. Now he can attempt to cross us up," she fussed as they crossed over the train platforms to catch another train. Twenty minutes later they ascended into a brisk December afternoon. Kitty sped back to the house.

When they entered they found the atmosphere had changed drastically from breakfast. Gone was the homey atmosphere of honey and heavenly biscuits. Now the air was charged with anger. Roosevelt paced for a moment, yelling about the breach of his privacy. Her parents were locked in battle in the living room. Davis stood close to the door holding Kitty's hand. She squeezed his hand and seemed to be considering her next move.

Yesenia sat almost dwarfed in an occasional chair, her head bowed and eyes closed. When she opened her eyes, Roosevelt rushed over and kneeled by her side. It turned out that Yesenia Franklin did have a voice, and the reporter's visit had released it. Since they stood so far away, the most Davis could make out was an occasional hiss from Yesenia. She reminded Davis of the phrase 'silent but deadly'. Davis knew she dealt deadly blows with every comment. Roosevelt could only whimper and reply with 'I'm sorry, 'Senia' or ' 'Senia, no.' This went on for several minutes until an outraged Yvette blew past them into the room.

Yvette verbally went for her father's jugular. "Your chickens have finally come home to roost. All the power you supposedly wield and you couldn't keep that reporter from coming to our home, upsetting my mother." Yvette hopped around the room. "I can't stand to be around you or live in this town any longer. I've got to get out of here. I just decided. Quanny and I are out of here. And I hope Mommy leaves you for good this time."

Kitty dropped Davis's hand and went to defend her client. "Yvette, stop it." She approached her sister. Davis watched carefully. Yvette hadn't struck him as a person of many words, certainly not as many as Kitty. Yvette might have spent her deck on Roosevelt. In his experience when people ran out of words in situations like this their next move was usually to hit. He stood alert, just in case.

His family argued, but nothing like this. His mother was a very loud yeller and his father could out yell her. There was an intensity to this situation like twenty years of conflict was about to come to a head. This was no place for him. He shouldn't bear witness to this kind of interaction. He probably should just go outside. Nevertheless he stayed glued. At first he reasoned that he was there to protect Kitty, but by the way she was besting her sister in a war of words, it was Yvette that needed protection. The sisters raged at each other about loyalty and loving their parents. Roosevelt moved to sit on the sofa with his head low. The congressman looked old and tired. After a moment, Yesenia rose and whispered, "Enough."

The room went still. Everyone held their breath and followed her every move. Without a backward glance she brushed past her husband and children. "Davis, I apologize that you had to see us at our worst," she said and swept up the stairs.

Roosevelt stomped off in the direction of his study. Within seconds Yvette flew past him and followed her mother upstairs. And without a glance Davis's way, Kitty ran after her father.

Davis took a seat in the living room and warred with himself. He was having a hard time with the image of Kitty running after her father without at least excusing herself from him. He'd come all this way to be with Kitty and she didn't have time to be with him. Was she even free to be with him? What bothered him most was the fact she didn't even seem to consider she had a choice.

As he sat he tried to convince himself that it was bad timing. Surely it couldn't be like this all the time. Maybe he'd just met Kitty during a bad cycle. Every job had its busy cycles. Was this thing with her father just one of those cyclic things?

But that didn't explain her rudeness or the way she seemed to forget he was there. Maybe he was wasting his time. Maybe Kitty was too wrapped up in her father's problems to recognize her own. He should get his things and go home. Too bad she didn't know that just one word from her and he would sit all night and wait while she worked with her father. Did he have to come all this way to see her true colors?

An hour later Yesenia Franklin descended the staircase, calm and regal, with Yvette and Quanny as attendants in tow. She was very civil when she offered him a ride to the airport in her Town Car. In the hour he'd sat there he'd just about decided to leave, since Kitty was lost to him, deep in a strategy session with her father.

Suddenly the doorbell rang and Kitty bolted from nowhere for the door.

Davis stretched and grinned, happy to wake up in Kitty's apartment. He sat up in bed and glanced around her bedroom. Everything around him was spa green and relaxing. Modern minimalist furniture with Japanese screens and bamboo plants created an atmosphere of calm. The room reminded him of a spa retreat rather than a room in someone's home. But he understood. Kitty needed this calming space. She'd even told him last night that this room was her sanctuary. She even had a calming water fountain in a corner.

He looked up at the ceiling and smiled, pleased with the decision he'd made yesterday. Just when he was about to leave the Franklin house, Kitty chose him. Without discussing it or looking back, Kitty walked out of her parents' house with him after she let the attorney called Uncle Tom in.

And just as on the night they'd met, she'd insisted that they have dinner at B. Smith's restaurant, take a crisp night stroll around the Washington Monument, and not speak about her father.

"Good morning, baby." She bounded into bed and snuggled up to him. As she worked her way under the covers, Phat Head woke up. "Get up and I'll take you out to breakfast before I get you to the airport."

"Umm, baby, I don't think I want to go anywhere now. Tell you what. I'll stay right here in bed and wait for you to come home every night. This is the most comfortable bed I've ever slept in. I don't want to move."

She settled in closer to him and whispered, "Get out of my bed."

Davis let out a belly laugh. "Girl, you don't know how much I love you."

"I know, but we can skip breakfast and you can show me again before it's time to leave." She kissed him slowly.

Davis whistled a little as he moved through security at Reagan National Airport. He was even happier now with his decision to stay with Kitty. They'd had a good time together last night, with the promise of more good times to come. Kitty managed to physically and emotionally reassure him that there was merit in their relationship. After doing an O.J. through the airport Davis just made his flight back to South Carolina.

His phone rang just as he arrived at his assigned gate.

"Davis." His mother sounded upset. "Charlie's back in the hospital. It may be the last time."

He found a seat and sat down as her words resonated. "I'm on my way home, Mom." That's how life was. Just when everything seemed to fall into place and you held happiness in your hand, something always happened.

Chapter 18

Kitty pushed the button to let down the car window to get a whiff of fresh South Carolina air. Twenty more miles and she'd roll into Rock Hill. She checked her mirrors and changed lanes. Twenty miles and home. Nineteen miles to Davis. A current of electricity tickled her chest. He'd been more than generous to forgive her despite what had happened earlier this week when he was in DC. To know she had been just steps away from losing him concerned her greatly. Bless God that Uncle Tom had rung that doorbell when he did.

Now all that was behind her and she was set to spend Christmas with Davis at home. This forgiveness thing was good, liberating. The other night they'd stayed on the phone until dawn talking. Things in their relationship were good but not perfect. They'd agreed she could rely on the power of forgiveness instead of the power of prayer since she wasn't ready to profess her faith. He was going to pray for their relationship to prosper. It all seemed so simple. Forgiveness was simple in concept, but complex in practice. But they were determined to work together. He'd also reminded her of the twelve tenets of the BMA church that he used to guide his life. She agreed to meditate on them since he couldn't ask her to pray.

Good God. Why was life set up this way? In every good thing there was some bad. She shook her head. "Perfect description of Daddy."

In spite of all the bad he'd done, she loved him. She changed lanes to pass an eighteen-wheeler.

"Mark off another one of his nine lives." Someway, somehow, the reporter had dropped the story. Kitty didn't know why or how and didn't care to ask. By some marvelous trick Toni's heart had softened and they'd come to terms. Daddy would see his son on some weekends, but no holidays. The tuition at Georgetown was paid. The full ride scholarship from the Congressional Black Caucus Foundation stood in spite of the investigation. Tom Ridgel had worked his magic and the ethics investigation had died.

She turned off her radio so she could process recent events in their lives. Yvette had started her new life in Boston. How could she do it? Yvette actually moved out of state so Reggie could share custody of their daughter? Now that Yvette had accepted Reggie's engagement, she seemed more settled. Maybe now she could move on and find herself a prince. But there was a little more to the story that Kitty was sure Yvette didn't know. She'd thought about telling her sister but decided it was best to keep out of that relationship, especially since she didn't want anyone in hers.

It was funny how Yvette had actually prophesied the outcome of her relationship with Reggie. Right after Quanny was born, Yvette had said she'd never forgive Reggie for leaving her while she was pregnant. And even after several major attempts at reconciliation things had never worked out between the two of them.

Kitty smiled. It was all about forgiveness. Thank God, Dena had forgiven her and she had her baby sister back. They even talked about working together once Dena finished law school. Kitty checked her speed and lifted her foot just a tad. They'd had lunch last week. For Christmas Dena forgave her for being their father's spy. Dena called it a rotten job but said she understood why she did it. And she joked that if they were going to practice law together Kitty would have to find a nicer client. By now Dena and her Levi were enjoying the holidays on the beach in sunny California. According to Dena, Levi's mother adored her; the race issue didn't bother her. Or Yesenia. The congressmen, however, were a different issue.

Her father had recently commissioned a poll, the results of which he shared with Congressman Stein. The response from their respective districts on interracial dating was not positive.

She laughed out loud. As much as she hated the corrupt, philandering, re-election hungry congressman, she loved her father. But she wasn't ready to forgive him for what he'd made her do. And after her last talk with her mother she was sure her mother wasn't going to forgive him again. She definitely needed to go see her mother in the morning.

Kitty didn't have it all worked out yet, but for the first time in her life she was grateful for her mother's advice. No one knew how Davis had hurt her with his words. It had been so hard for her to hear and attempt to live up to his demands that she stand on her own. Thank God, Davis only sought her good. So she was free to bask in the well wishes of her family for landing a majestic black prince. Except for Daddy. Even Mama Cat was ready to relent and come to church on Sunday to hear Davis sing. That man really was almost perfect.

She shrugged and pressed on the gas. Davis was a saint for putting up with her debilitating headaches, high workload, her father, and her mouth. Only two more things to do and she'd be free to enjoy the holidays. Deliver the box of Christmas cards for her father and keep her mother solid on the promise not to file for divorce until after the election.

She barked a voice command into her cell phone. When Davis answered she blurted, "I'm almost home."

"Tell me what you mean by 'almost home'?"

She checked the mirrors and noted her own broad smile at his low sexy voice. "I'll be at home when I'm with you."

"Well, all right. I just wanted to know how far out you were."

"Oh, I'm passing the farmers' market right now."

"Then I better turn around. I was going over to the church for an anniversary committee meeting. I wasn't expecting you until after two. Baby, you need to slow down. Rock Hill's finest would love to pull you over."

"Yeah, you're right." She lifted her foot. "You can go ahead to the church meeting. I don't want to keep you from your deacon duties." The board had voted him in a few days ago. "I've got something to do for Daddy, then I can meet you at the house." She glanced over at the box of envelopes on the passenger seat, Daddy's special Christmas envelopes. Task one, get this box to Glynnis.

Daddy was always a generous Santa, and this year's envelopes looked fairly thick. She'd learned years ago not to question where the money to stuff the Christmas envelopes came from and not to deposit the cash into her checking account or make any sudden large purchases.

"Does this have anything to do with the envelopes Glynnis has been talking about for the last month?"

"Uh-huh."

"Kitty, I really don't want you involved with anything like that."

My good, decent, honest man.

"I don't know what you're talking about. And as an officer of the court all I know is that my client asked me to deliver Christmas cards to his staff."

He groaned. "If one of those envelopes is for me, I don't want it."

"Don't worry, I know how you feel. There's only a Christmas card for you from my mother. Daddy gave me all the money." She snapped her lips shut. She shouldn't have said that. What if her conversation were recorded? There were some powerful forces seeking to bring her father down. They wouldn't hesitate to tap her phone. Her father had actually given Davis a tidy sum. She'd already spent hours trying to figure out a way to get it to him without his notice. She frowned. Too bad he'd rejected her offer to spend the holidays on a private island in the Caribbean.

"Just passing the high school," she said cheerily.

"I'll meet you at home in a minute."

"Okay. See you at home."

"Sounds good to me."

Home, home with Davis, the only place in the world she wanted to be. Two weeks pretending she was Mrs. Davis Thornton. It would be their trial marriage, since they'd never spent more than three days together. And it was going to be quite a chore since the trial Mrs. Thornton was expected to go to church and behave as a proper deacon's wife, which meant keeping her mouth shut. Maybe she could give his Christmas bonus to the church. It would be a sizable donation from the newest deacon. No, the church would no doubt report the contribution to the IRS. She signaled for the exit to take her home.

Several hours later Kitty lay in the shelter of Davis's arms and yawned. "How long have I been asleep?" She rolled over. "I guess the drive took a lot more out of me than I thought."

Davis shifted. "I'll call Mama and tell her we won't come out to the house for dinner."

She stretched her arms over her head. "You want me to cook?" Mrs. Thornton would cook.

"Uh, no, but I do want you to tell me what you think about this room."

She sat up in bed and glanced around her room, the first of what Davis had called her many Christmas presents. When she walked into the house he'd led her to this second bedroom, decorated just for her. The walls were a soft lilac and the bedding had what Davis called big girl pink and purple swirls. There was even a metal crown thing on the wall. That was about all she saw before she jumped him.

"It's very nice. I like it."

Davis sat up on the side of the bed. "This is your room. Anytime you feel you need to have some privacy, come in here."

Kitty stood up on her knees and wrapped her arms around Davis's neck and kissed him. "Same goes for you."

"No, Kitty. This is your space. I hope everything's wrapped up. But if you need to work come in here and I won't disturb you."

He brushed her forehead with his upper lip. "I'm looking forward to the two weeks together. I'm going to be working to get you to stay." He kissed her forehead. "Why don't you relax? I'll fix us some dinner."

"No." She struggled to stand. "Shouldn't I be doing that?"

"That's all right, Kitty. I'm too hungry to eat take-out tonight."

After dinner Kitty lounged on the sofa and stared at the Christmas tree. "Good thing you don't have much furniture. That tree is taking up most of the space in here." She glanced around his Spartan living room as she mulled over how to decorate the space. She held enough money of his to buy some nice leather furniture and art work to complete this room.

"I got a big tree 'cause I'm having a big Christmas." Davis sat next to her.

The twinkle of the multicolored tree lights bathed the sparsely furnished room in a homey light. "And are all those presents for me?" she asked.

"No."

Her lip poked out.

"But most of them are."

Kitty grinned and snuggled into the safety of his arms. She took a deep breath. "Umm, that tree smells so good, kinda minty."

"That's a South Carolina blue sapphire. Smells like home."

Kitty took another breath and inhaled deeply of Davis's scent. "You smell like home to me." An insistent buzz from her BlackBerry interrupted the still of the evening.

Reluctantly, she stood and walked over to pick her phone up from the foyer table. "Sorry, I thought I turned that off." She checked the caller ID, glanced back with a frown. "I need to take this. Hello?"

On her line was Yurgay, a seventeen-year-old Russian computer hacker who worked for the CIA. When Tee couldn't find the identity of the blog owner dedicated to destroying her father, her father had used his connections. His connection had referred them to Yurgay. When she spoke to him yesterday she'd taken it as a youthful boast when he promised to have the name of the site's owner within twenty-four hours. She hadn't expected to hear from him until after the New Year.

Chapter 19

Hours passed as she sat in his arms on the worn leather sofa. A knot of grief throbbed in her chest. First she'd moaned, "No, no." Then, "It's not true." Finally, silently, she accepted Yurgay's report. Through it all a concerned Davis sat by her side.

"Is everyone in the family okay? Did something happen to your parents? Mama Cat? Quanny?" he asked.

She shook her head.

He let it go for a minute. "Dena arrived safely in California, right?"

She didn't answer.

"Kitty, please. Whatever it is, let me in."

She drew in closer to him. She needed his strength. But this she couldn't share with him. The genesis of a headache formed in the back of her skull. She'd need to get up and take something soon. But right now she couldn't move. Couldn't bring herself to speak. If she were at home with her family, they'd all call her silence a Christmas miracle. Kitty Franklin unable to speak! Her sisters would be overjoyed. She sniffled. All she wanted was to melt into Dave's loving care. But Yurgay's precise, careful, broken English continually pounded in her brain. 'Do you wish the full report sent via email or courier?'

It wasn't who owned the website that upset her. Just as she'd suspected, it wasn't the radical black nationalist running against her father in the next election. It was a political action committee made up of some key South Carolina republicans. It shouldn't have taken any special services to uncover this. What upset her was the holiday posting of her mother's divorce petition. The dark mist of guilt and betrayal invaded her and her sight dimmed.

"Kitty?" Davis shifted her weight from his shoulder. His tone intensified. "Baby, this is killin' me, I've got to know. Does this have anything to do with your father?"

What would he say if she told him that she had drafted her mother's divorce petition? And how would he react if she told him that her mother had betrayed her? The divorce petition was supposed to remain a secret. Her mother had agreed not to file for divorce until after the election. She couldn't tell him any of this. He'd lose all respect for her and her mother.

"Kitty," he growled, untangling himself and standing.

First she flopped over. Then she righted herself on the sofa. She tried to focus as he stood by the Christmas tree. Her eyes clouded. Beyond her classical conception of a small white angel, before her was a true angel. The silent twinkling of the tiny lights haloed his frame. Big, black, and by far the most loving being she'd ever encountered. She tried to open her mouth. But only a low moan came out.

His voice rose from the darkness. "I had planned...." he started in a low, measured tone.

She focused on his frame as he kneeled beside the tree pulling through the presents.

"I had planned to ask you to marry me tonight." His voice went up an octave. He paused, then stood and placed a small box in his pocket. "But I see now that we're nowhere near ready for that."

She covered her mouth. What had she done?

"The woman I want to marry is able to share everything with me, good and bad," he yelled and stalked out of the room. At the entrance to the hall he stopped. "Whatever it is, I bet you're itching to call and tell your daddy."

She lay speechless on the couch.

Kitty couldn't quite remember if she'd stumbled her way into her bedroom or if an angel had assisted. She rolled over to check the clock. On the nightstand stood a glass of water, her prescriptions, and her BlackBerry. Davis in his loving kindness had cared for her, again. She stared up at the ceiling.

Davis's words rang in her ear. She wasn't itching to call her father. Her father would never forgive her for what she'd done. Together she and her mother had dealt him a political death blow. She sent Twanna a text to try and figure how those papers came to be posted. She'd go see her mother and ask why.

Despite his kindness the tone in his voice last night had been clear. She rolled over onto the cold side of the bed. She'd destroyed her parents' marriage and lost her chance at happiness. How was she supposed to live with this on her heart? The tears flowed. She couldn't share this with her sisters or Twanna. She wouldn't breathe a word of this to Davis. Alone, with no one to cry out to, she pleaded, "Oh, God, why me? Why do I have to pay such a heavy price?"

She covered her face with a pillow as Davis stirred about the house. Enjoying the sounds of his moving around the house in the morning as he prepared for his morning run was supposed to be her reward. They had an agreement. The trial Mrs. Thornton didn't have to get out of bed to cook him breakfast. In fact, she didn't have to do anything, not even go to church on Sunday. He'd given her the option to come hear him sing today at the Center. She pressed the pillow closer to her face.

But long term there was something else he required of her. He'd asked her to consider her loyalties. More than once he'd said for their relationship to prosper he needed to believe her fidelity would be to him. Last night he'd been ready to trust her, to ask her to be his wife. And she couldn't open her big mouth and tell him why she drew up divorce papers for her mother. Now she'd never be Mrs. Davis Thornton. "Why me, Lord?" She cried out again to the God Davis had asked she try to believe in.

She glanced over at the nightstand and the glass of water, a simple sign of his love. He deserved better than connection to her and her family.

She lay still and listened. Davis was still in the house. Given the hour, it was getting a little late for a run. She turned her head toward the door when he knocked and the door creaked open. "You need to pack your things and go to your mother's house today, while I'm at work."

Davis was a bit off balance when he arrived at the Center two hours later. He should have passed up the pancake breakfast he'd just eaten. Glynnis sat at her desk rifling through a box of envelopes. Before he could get past her she whooped and praised the Lord.

"You just missed Cousin Kitty," she cried as she held up another envelope.

She's already on the job for her father.

"Yeah." He strode past her into his office.

Davis plopped down at his desk and fired up his computer. There wasn't much to do today outside of singing for the seniors at the luncheon. Kitty had planned to attend. Not to represent her father, but to stand with him. One of the tasks she thought she should attend to as the trial Mrs. Thornton. He rubbed his temples. "What were we thinking?" he asked himself.

Reason was quick to respond. We were definitely moving too fast.

No, never, not when they're giving it up, fat boy. Phat Head got his shot in.

He looked up and Glynnis stood before him. "You don't look so great, boss. Kitty talk you to death or wear you out last night?" She twirled a lock of her blonde weave around her finger. "Come to think of it, Kitty didn't look so hot when she blew through here a while ago. Trouble in paradise?"

He cut his eyes at her and picked up a stack of mail.

"Look, I just called the judge and he wants me to run this out to his place right away." She twirled a fat envelope around in the air.

He looked up from his stack. "Now? The senior Christmas party starts at eleven."

"Yeah, I know. I'll be right back. The judge's been waiting. He said Cousin Rosey promised he'd have it today, this morning. He's trying to get to his house on Hilton Head for the holidays."

Powerless to act against the express wishes of Roosevelt Franklin, he waved her on.

"By the way, if Penny comes by, tell him his envelope is at the reception desk."

His brow furrowed. "You'd leave something like that at the main desk?"

"Yeah, for Penny. It ain't nothin" but a card."

He smirked. "And Penny could probably use the cash more than the judge."

She took a step into his office. "And if you'd taken the time to get to know Penny, you'd know why his envelope is empty."

He rubbed his eyes. The last thing he needed this morning was a dose of Glynnis's sass. Taking the time to get to know Penny, the Center's well-respected maintenance man, was on his agenda, something that Kitty had suggested. "What's his story, anyway?"

"Real quick, Penny's a good man."

"I know that."

"Well, 'bout ten years back Penny had a problem with gamecock fighting. He was real good at training them chickens. His game got popular and some of them white boys from down the road started coming 'round here. Of course they got mad 'cause they lost a ton of money. They started some stuff one night and Penny had to knock a few of 'em on their ass. And you know that South Carolina ain't changed that much. It took the congressman and the judge to keep him out of the pen. After that Penny said Cousin Rosey never needed to do anything else for him. So he only takes his pay, which he earns, and accepts a card at Christmas, but that's mainly for his wife. She likes to have the congressman's signature." Glynnis stepped closer and flipped two cards onto his desk. "These are yours. One's addressed to your mother. It's awful thin. What you doing wrong?"

"No, ma'am." His voice sounded weary. "I don't want anything to do with what's going on. I told Kitty to keep me out of that."

"That's on you. Be right back." She bounced away in her cherry red pinafore and green elf shoes. If he weren't so mad he'd laugh at how ridiculous she looked. Davis shook his head and wondered what Kitty would say about Glynnis's outfit. He picked up the cards she'd left and turned them over in his hand. The heavy linen envelopes were written in an even, considered, ladylike penmanship. Probably Mrs. Franklin's.

"For all we don't know about Kitty," he spoke aloud to himself, "we do know her handwriting." His very modern and electronically connected Kitty sent him letters and cards, at least three times a week via the good old U.S. postal service.

Despite her famous mouth she was better at expressing her heart in writing. All of her letters were signed 'I love you'. He sifted through the mail on his desk for something from her. Her non-verbal communications always spoke straight to his heart. He raced through the remaining mail.

All that mouth and last night she couldn't talk. He shook his head and thought over the many nights when she sat up with him over the phone or webcam and just listened to him. It was a very pleasant surprise to find out that she could silently listen to his troubles and when the time was right, give him the most patient, kind, and loving advice, such as asking him to make time to get to know Penny. His mustache twitched.

Even during their worst times she'd advised him to hire a private attorney to go over his employment contract. If it weren't for her, he might have gone on thinking he was the executive director of the Center instead of just director. And he'd be out about ten thousand dollars a year. Something else Roosevelt Franklin had tried to slip by him. She'd advised him to amend the number and ask for more money when he shared with her his concerns about the deliberate misprint on the contract.

He reached the end of the stack. Nothing from Kitty. His mustached lip turned down. He opened the card Glynnis had passed him. A foil and parchment greeting wishing him and Kitty a wonderful and restful holiday season; it was signed by Yesenia. It was a nice card. It looked like something Kitty might have picked out. And maybe she had. "Lady, I do like your style."

He put the second card addressed to his family in his briefcase. He knew better than to open his mother's mail.

"Let me go out here and make sure everything is in order," he said out loud. Anything to keep busy and resist the urge to call home and ask her to stay. No. There was something lacking in the relationship. And he'd moved too fast.

"Because I didn't want her to get away." He stretched. The knot in his hamstring pinged in regret that he had not gone out for a run this morning. A good, long run would have helped him work out his frustration and maybe lose a little of the weight he'd gained since moving home. He stretched his legs out and found a small glimmer of hope. Kitty could be stubborn; maybe she wouldn't leave.

After a short stroll around the Center, he was back in his office staring at his phone. Glynnis had everything in order for the luncheon. She was good at her job. Nothing else to do, he picked up the phone, then set it back in its cradle. He wasn't going to call her. "Let's take a walk down to the maintenance deck and have a cup of coffee with Penny," he said to himself.

A few hours later he scanned the ballroom full of local seniors decked out in their Christmas finery for the annual luncheon. His Christmas wish was that Kitty would pull herself together and boldly stroll in, just in time to claim her place beside him. No, whatever happened on that call last night had truly hurt her. For all her bravado, his Kitty was a sweet, sensitive girl and she needed him to stand by her. His love for her should have trumped his anger and instead of asking her to leave, he should have stayed by her side last night. All night if that was what it took, whether she shared with him what had happened or not. He should have stayed at home with her today. But if she truly loved and needed him, wouldn't she want to let him share her burdens?

The children from the day care center filed onto the stage and began to recite their Christmas poem. He rocked back on his heels to the cadence of their Christmas story. Forward and back. His relationship with Kitty and the congressman had a similar ebb and flow. One minute he'd be totally disgusted with Roosevelt for his nefarious activities and in the next he'd be filled with admiration for the man. Penny's story was evidence of the lengths that Roosevelt would go to protect one of his constituents. On Penny's behalf Roosevelt had broken a state law and housed him in Virginia until it was safe for Penny to return home.

He swayed forward and understood Kitty. She was protecting someone. Probably her father. *There's dichotomy in all of us. Dichotomy, I've got to ruminate on that.* He rocked back on his heels.

"Now our Center director, Mr. Davis Thornton," Glynnis squealed.

He moved forward at Glynnis's direction. She was doing a decent job today as program hostess.

"He's gonna sing for y'all."

He cringed at her grammar. Dichotomy again: great event planner, awful public speaker. He scanned the room one more time; maybe Kitty had slipped in. He held up his hand in a signal for the pianist not to play. He'd planned to sing O Holy Night, but the melody was beyond his reach today. Instead he offered an acappella rendition of "Have Yourself a Merry Little Christmas." Dichotomy. He was nowhere near merry.

After singing, he joined Penny and the rest of the maintenance staff for lunch. Turned out that Penny was also a funny man. The cheer did his heart good. Reluctantly he rose and left the table before dessert was served to make his rounds. He worked the room diagonally, saving one particular table for last.

He took a deep breath to summon his courage and approach Mama Cat. He shook a few hands of church members and other seniors as he moved closer to Catherine Franklin, senior.

"Hello, Mama Cat. How are you enjoying the luncheon?"

She tapped his lower leg with her cane. "Mama Cat is a family name."

"Yes, ma'am, please excuse me." He stood up a little straighter and took a step back. "Mrs. Franklin, ma'am, may I ask ..."

"No, you may not ask me anything, but you can tell me why my granddaughter always comes back from your house crying. Now sit down. I'll strain my neck trying to look up at you."

He wanted to crack a smile. Kitty's sharp tongue was a direct inheritance from her grandmother. He pulled a chair from an emptying table and sat forward to listen. "Yes, ma'am."

It was a quick chastisement on courtship and how people took things slower back in her day.

"Yes, ma'am." He started his request after she indicated a willingness to listen to him speak. "I agree with you and in the absence of Kitty's parents, may I ask your permission to come by your house to see Kitty? I'd like to take her to my mother's house for dinner this evening, and of course I'll bring her home tonight at whatever time you say."

The old woman drew herself up and hugged her cane. "No."

He leaned back. It would have hurt less if she'd hit him again.

"Now where's that Glynnis? I'm ready to go home."

"Yes, ma'am." He stood slowly and searched the room for Glynnis.

"Son," she tapped his leg again, "Kitty's gone back to DC."

By mid-morning Kitty had hit the road. A short stop by her mother's house had ended in a rush of tears. Her mother had gone Christmas shopping. Her grandmother would have worried her to death if she'd stayed another minute in that house. What would the divorce do to the relationship that her mother and grandmother shared? Those two hadn't always gotten along. It was only after Quanny was born that Mama Cat warmed up to her daughter-in-law. Mama Cat was a stalwart with regard to any perceived threat to her son. For over twenty years she hadn't stepped foot in her home church because she thought Roosevelt might get in trouble for participating in the civil rights movement. Considering what her grandmother might do to her, Kitty sped out of Rock Hill and didn't stop for gas until she reached the Virginia state line.

Along the way she screamed and cursed her father. No matter what her mother had done she could forgive her, because her father was the root of all the trouble. He'd driven his wife to the divorce by being a lying, cheating, womanizing snake. The final straw had apparently come last week when the reporter from the Post came to the house. When her mother left that day she'd checked into the Washington Hilton, instead of returning to Rock Hill. Two days later Yesenia called and Kitty met her for lunch.

Yesenia confided in her that there wasn't a single attorney in the District she could trust. Without speaking a negative word about her husband she pleaded with Kitty to help her file for divorce.

As a daughter Kitty understood her mother's decision to seek a divorce. As her father's attorney and political consultant she asked Yesenia to delay taking any action until after the election. Her mother agreed. She didn't want to destroy her husband. Then Yesenia fell apart. She cried for over an hour about wanting the divorce to preserve her own sanity.

Her mother had appeared so fragile that Kitty decided to stop being her father's daughter and help her mother.

"Why, Mommy?" She wiped away the tears and drove on.

Twenty miles later she slammed her fist down on the steering wheel. "Damn you, Daddy. You destroyed your marriage and now my relationship. God, I wish I had the nerve to call a press conference and tell it all!"

She jumped at the blare of the horn from an eighteen-wheeler and she straightened her vehicle on the road. Her head pounded. She gripped the wheel and drove on. Further away from her future she sped. The deeper into Virginia she drove the dimmer her vision.

"What good was my big mouth to me last night? I should have told Davis all. He wouldn't believe it. Hell, I barely believe it. I actually drafted a divorce petition for my mother." She'd drawn up the paperwork only because her mother couldn't rest without having it. It was like her sunshine fund. Yesenia needed to hold something, some card in her poker game with her husband. She'd agreed to hold the paperwork and not to file for divorce until after the election. Kitty racked her brain to trying to figure out what could have happened to make her mother go back on her word.

She reached over to accept a phone call from Twanna. It took Tee less than three hours to figure out that her mother hadn't betrayed her. Yesenia had just been careless. Her mother was unaware that the practice of celebrity trash picking had come to Washington. In truth, the practice probably originated there. There was an ex-lobbyist who reportedly paid hotel maids big money for the waste bins from certain hotel rooms. When

Yesenia tossed the divorce papers in the trash can before she checked out of the Hilton, she didn't know that her trash was being sold.

Kitty leaned forward as the road narrowed. Kitty signaled to change lanes and slowed down. Twanna's call lifted her burdens a little; her faith in her mother was restored. It took a hundred miles to convince herself there was nothing she could say to restore Davis's faith in her.

"Yvette told me my mouth would mess me up. It's funny, but not opening my mouth did me in."

She scooted up closer to the wheel and tightened her grip. "Focus on the white lines, just focus on the white lines," she repeated as she drove. Focus on the white lines, the guidelines. She lightened the pressure on the accelerator. Cars whizzed by on her left. Guidelines? Wasn't she following God's guidelines? Honor thy mother and father. "Haven't I done that?" she yelled at God. "I did exactly what my father and mother asked of me." She caught a flash of light coming from the rear. "Go around," she yelled and slowed down. The light dimmed. She rolled on for another mile or so before flashing blue lights crept into her now limited vision. She pressed on the brake, rolled to a stop, and turned her car off. An overhead voice requested she pull off the road.

"Ohh," she screamed as sirens blared. She didn't move. She sat and waited. Within minutes twin sirens wailed around her and a car pulled up alongside her.

"Pull over off the road," the overhead voice instructed again.

"Oh, God, help me." She felt her way to turn on the ignition so she could roll the window down.

The overhead voice boomed, "Ma'am, you're putting a lot of people at risk here. Pull over to the side, off the highway. Now!"

She felt the presence at her window. "Do you hear me, miss?"

She nodded.

"Can you see me?"

"No," she whimpered.

"I've got a medical and request backup," he said into what she assumed was a radio.

She could perceive only a shadowy impression of the military khaki of a state trooper's uniform.

"Miss, keep calm. We're here to help you."

Moments later, Kitty sat on the passenger side of her BMW somewhere between South Carolina and Maryland. Her feet dangled out the door. The smell of car exhaust and dust swirled around her. A female officer that she could not quite see kneeled beside her.

"Girlfriend, if it wasn't for the grace of God... Do you realize you came to a dead stop on the highway? He's looking out for you. Do you know that your car was surrounded for several miles by three eighteen-wheelers? Girl, they had a hedge of protection around you! If I weren't in this uniform, I'd shout."

The expressive officer reminded Kitty of Twanna. Under ordinary circumstances she'd have something smart to say. Today she only bowed her head lower.

"You have a huge angel watching over you. Traffic's slowed and backed up for miles. And here you sit, just as calm as can be. And I thank God for that."

Kitty shook. *What should I thank God for? My family? Or that I had a man like Davis, even though I lost him?* She bowed her head, cried, and thanked God for her life. It had to be God's protection because everything now was dark around her.

The officer covered her hands. "It's all right. Everything's made safe, you're safe. I'll wait with you until your transport comes."

From her tone and word choice Kitty knew she was speaking to a sista. "My father's a congressman. I'll make sure he takes care of you."

"I'm just doing my job. But can you give me your father's phone number? So we can call him."

"I don't know it." She lifted her tear-stained face. She had tomes of facts, rumors, and personal truths about her father stored in her brain, but she didn't know his phone number. "I don't know his number. I don't know anyone's number. They're all in my phone. It dropped on the floor a while back." She lowered her head and cradled it in her hands. "Can you turn those sirens off?"

She stood outside her car while the officer retrieved her phone.

"Call my assistant Tee," she said.

The screeching sirens were replaced by the ambient sounds of cars rolling along, happy people no doubt headed to spend the holidays with family. She'd been one of those happy speeders yesterday. Now less than a day later she was out on the road struggling against darkness.

"We're ready." The sista trooper guided her by her arm. "I'll walk with you to the ambulance. Don't you worry about anything. I got your purse and put most of the stuff that was spilled on the floor back in it. I'm going to take the rest of your personal effects into custody and your car will be impounded. Listen, Twanna's on her way, but it'll take her a few hours. She said Davis is closer. She wants to know if we should call him."

Kitty stopped and dug her heels into the roadside gravel. "No, no." She waved her hands through the air.

"Now don't start getting feisty with me."

Kitty stood for a moment before she allowed herself to be gently nudged forward. With the officer's assistance she moved toward the waiting ambulance.

"Are you sure?" the officer asked once more.

"He asked me to leave."

Chapter 20

Kitty sat up in the hospital bed. As if changing position in her hospital bed could alter her thoughts. Visions of herself in the future without Davis had tortured her all morning. That Terri Texas had probably already moved in on him. She was the good church-going type, and he deserved a nice wife. She tried to shut out the images of Davis with Terri. She wanted to call him. Contact him one last time and ask him to forgive her immaturity and wish him well. She owed him that. In the short time they were together he'd taught her about the power of forgiveness and shift. He'd even helped restore her faith in God. She had so much to say to him she'd started collecting her thoughts on some hospital chart paper. Writing out her thoughts and true feelings was challenging yet therapeutic.

"Kitty, girl, you know you see me standing over here."

She turned her head in the direction of her faithful Twanna. Tee had dropped everything, including an NFL lineman, on Christmas Eve to help her.

"I can't see you, but I can smell that knockoff Dolce and Gabanna cologne you bathed in."

Twanna hooted and moved toward her bed.

"And thank God my vision's too blurry to see whatever that is you're wearing from the House of Dereon."

"My girl is back." Tee reached down and hugged her. "Stop playing, you know you can see me and you know you want these boots I've got on."

Kitty laughed and took in the sharp patchwork leather boots Tee wore. Her father had been generous to her assistant, too.

"Listen, Kitty, your parents went to get coffee so I don't have much time to talk. So just keep that mouth of yours shut for a minute."

She blinked and tried to focus on Tee's face. When she saw Tee's expression, she closed her eyes. Her physical vision grew clearer every day, but emotionally there were some things she didn't wish to see.

"Kitty. Are you real sure that man doesn't love you?"

"Tee," she groaned. "I can't deal with that now. Daddy said all I have to do is focus on getting out of here."

Twanna stepped back. "Don't even mention your father to me."

Since the arrival of her parents at the hospital, Twanna and her father had been at odds. From what Kitty could tell, the conflict had started when Twanna first mentioned that Davis called her. Her father blew up and confiscated all of Kitty's electronic devices: cell phone, netbook, and iPod. She'd effectively been cut off from the world—except for Tee, who'd become her connector. Tee and the pad of notebook paper she kept hidden under her pillow.

"Kitty, I've got to tell you Davis keeps calling. Just about every day he leaves a message. He sounds so pitiful I just can't keep putting him off."

Kitty moaned.

"I haven't really talked to him because your father threatened me. And I need my job. But I did text him yesterday to say you're okay."

Kitty flopped down. "Well, the next time he calls, talk to him. Tell him I'm fine and not to call again. He'll leave you alone. He's just nice like that."

"Who's nice like what?" her father's voice boomed from across the room.

Twanna turned and set herself for another confrontation. "I was letting Kitty know that Davis called. Again."

"I told that big black bastard to stop contacting you. I'm real close to the final straw with you both," Roosevelt yelled at Twanna.

"Rosey, stop." Her mother placed a hand on her husband's shoulder. "You'll upset Kitty." Her parents had rushed from opposite directions to help her.

Kitty drew a deep breath and sat up in bed. "Daddy." Kitty's voice reached its usual timbre for the first time in days. She cleared her throat. "Don't you threaten Twanna, she works for me. And don't disrespect Lou ever again."

"Who?"

"Davis's mother. When you call him that you're casting aspersions on his mother, and I can't let you do that."

"Okay, okay, counselor. I'll give you that." Roosevelt waved his hand and flashed his campaign smile at the strength in her voice. "You sound good today, Kitten." His high-watt smile faded. "I don't want that boy bothering you. He's the cause of all of this."

Kitty shifted in the bed. "No, Daddy, he's not."

Roosevelt glared at her. "I don't care what you say. I know more about him than you think. He's not the prince charming you want everyone to believe."

"Rosey, stop," Yesenia pleaded.

"Well, he ain't." Roosevelt stomped over to the window.

"Kitty, girl, I'm out. I'll be back to see you later. Peace."

Kitty watched her assistant and best girlfriend sashay from the room. She closed her eyes so she wouldn't have to look at either of her parents. Her legs began to shake. "What are you trying to say, Daddy?"

"Nothing, Kitten," he muttered.

Her mother rushed to her side. "We don't need to get into that now. Right, Rosey?" Her mother picked up her hand and gave it a little squeeze. "I've almost got the doctors convinced to let you come home."

Beyond the cheerful face Yesenia tried to present, she'd been tense and unusually chatty since she arrived.

"Yeah, Kitten. Tomorrow we'll take you home." Her father stood on the opposite side of the bed and held her other hand. "We'll get you home and take care of you."

Her father kept emphasizing the we, knowing that the only reason Yesenia agreed to return to Washington was to help Kitty. Her mother wanted to take her to Rock Hill to recuperate, but Kitty had protested.

"I'm going to take care of you, Kitten. That's what a man is supposed to do." Her father squeezed her hand.

Kitty looked from her father to her mother, then closed her eyes. She didn't want to see either of them. "What's that, Daddy? I'm a princess and you are the knight in shining armor that's going to protect me?" She huffed. "No, it's the other way around, isn't it? I protected you...." Tears flowed out of her shut lids. "Neither of you should have asked me to get in between your lies and secrets."

She stopped and opened her eyes. She glanced over at her mother's tense shoulders.

Roosevelt blew out the breath he'd held while she spoke. "We don't need to get into all of this here."

Yesenia dropped her hand and stepped over to the visitor's chair. "No, Roosevelt, let her speak her peace. And you don't have to hold anything back, Catherine. I am very much aware of all your father's done."

Her mother, who never wished to hear a harsh word about any man and who never spoke a harsh word about her husband, didn't deserve her wrath. Even when Kitty was drawing up the divorce petition her mother had insisted that she not use any language that would denigrate him.

A cool breeze filtered to the room. Kitty inhaled the scent of fresh linen.

"No, Mommy. I've made my case."

"Then, my dearest daughter," her father squeezed her hand, "let me conclude this matter. And I hope you can take what I'm about to say in love. You're fired."

She inhaled again. Good.

"Kitten, if you want me to, when you're ready I'll help you find another job or set you up in a private practice, anything you want. Just use this time now to focus on yourself. On getting well. And someday, I hope you'll think about forgiving your poor father."

Her father pulled her hand towards his face and kissed her palm. There was an uncharacteristic sadness in his eyes. Roosevelt turned and left the room.

Her mother whispered, "I hope you'll forgive me, too. I should have been more careful with those papers. And I should have put a stop to your working for your father years ago. When you started, I didn't realize that he'd involve you in his personal business to the extent that he has. But like his affairs, it was another one of those secrets he kept from me until it was too late or about to destroy him. Kitty, whatever your father's done, you need to know two things. I've forgiven him. And you need to know how very much he loves you."

"Mommy, why bother and forgive him again?"

Kitty had a feeling the answer lay somewhere in the faith she now shared with her mother.

"It's what's required."

She took in another cleansing breath. Would Davis feel required to forgive her? Since her mother was being unusually chatty, she asked another question. "Why now?"

Yesenia sighed. "When that reporter came to the door I was at a point where I felt that your father had stopped listening to me. And I've known for years that you girls no longer heard my voice. I can't tell you how lonely and isolated I felt from all of you."

Kitty's heart softened. Until she met Davis, she'd felt the same way about being her father's secret keeper. It was isolating.

Kitty sat up and turned toward her mother. "Mommy, I'm so sorry for everything I've done. I hope someday you can forgive me for being such a poor daughter?"

"Kitty, you're a wonderful daughter and I've already forgiven you," Yesenia sighed. "It's not your fault, Kitty. Nothing that has happened is your fault."

Kitty wiped away a tear. "Mommy, how did you do it for so many years?"

Yesenia lowered her head. "Kitty, a marriage is between two people. And as long as your father and I could resolve our issues and agree to stay together, I truly believed that it didn't matter what anyone else thought. But to some extent I should have included you and your sisters in the circle of our marriage. I hate the nasty toll this has taken on my girls, mostly on you."

"I'll be all right."

"I know you will, Kitty. I admire you so much as a woman. Your strength and spunk inspire me. You may look like me, but your spirit is all from Mama Cat."

"Mommy, what are we going to say to Mama Cat? You two seem so close now."

"We are, and don't you worry about your grandmother. If I let her travel she'd be here with us now."

"I thought she'd be mad at me."

"Your grandmother loves you unconditionally. Just never slip and say a negative word about your father in her presence. We owe her that respect. But don't think for a minute that she doesn't know all about him." Her mother sat back in the chair and half smiled. "Not long after Yvette was born I suspected that Roosevelt was sneaking around and I tried to talk to Mama about it. She told me off good. And she was right, that time. It turned out that he was innocent. The way she lit into me, I'll never forget it. We didn't fully reconcile until well after Quanny was born." Her smile deepened. "I love her, but Mama can hold a grudge."

Kitty relaxed a bit. "I know. Did she tell you she was going to church?" She stopped as her mind raced forward to the end of the statement. Mama Cat was to attend church with her and Davis during the holidays.

"Yes, baby. I know."

They sat in silence for a while. For the first time in years she'd had an honest conversation with her mother. Over the past few weeks she'd gained a better understanding of her mother, a woman who'd weathered many storms in her marriage and could still face her family and the public with poise. It had to be love and the power of forgiveness.

She glanced over at her mother as she sat in contemplation or prayer. When and how had she become so serene? Her no-drama mama hadn't always been that way. An old memory of her mother chastising her for smarting off flashed in her mind. That was followed by a more recent memory when their mother laid into Dena for having sex in public places. Yesenia hadn't lost her cool in years, but she sure gave it to Dena that day. She glanced over at her mother sitting so ladylike and still.

They sat for a while longer. Kitty thought about her sisters and how she longed to see them both. Dena would come back from California in a few days and Yvette was coming in the morning. She had to wait in Boston while Quanny spent Christmas with Reggie. She remembered her mother's gentle correction of Yvette. She had never allowed Yvette to denigrate Reggie to the point that he couldn't come around the family. Their mother didn't deserve the nickname they'd given her. They were wrong to think she didn't have any backbone. There was more depth to their mother than they'd realized.

"Mommy, are you really going to Reggie's wedding?"

"Absolutely! My Quanny's going to be the flower girl. I'm going to sit in the front pew of that cathedral with Reggie's mother in my pearls and St. John suit and after I'll spend a few days in Boston with Yvette. Just in case she needs me."

Forgiveness and love welled up in Kitty's chest. And there was one more question she needed to ask.

"Mommy? Are you going through with the divorce?"

"Kitty, I don't know. If anything good has come out of this situation it's that I've found somebody to talk to." Yesenia stood up to stretch.

"Who?"

"Your father. Now change the subject, Kitty."

Kitty closed her eyes. A marriage really was between two people, and she was no longer going to deal with the complexities of her parent's situation. Her father held his congressional seat because of their mother's long-suffering. It was Yesenia's spirit of forgiveness that had kept their marriage afloat and the family intact. Forgiveness was more sustaining than love.

Chapter 21

It seemed like months instead of days since Kitty left. Davis lay across the bed in her room belting out Luther's "A House Is Not a Home" for the hundredth time. "That's right, Luther, this house ain't a home."

For days now he'd wandered through his house in the dark, sharing his sorrow with Luther in song. He hadn't asked her to leave the state, just to go to her mother's house. But in her immaturity she'd fled like a child back to her daddy. She'd almost killed herself trying to drive back to DC. He thanked God again for her life and mentally kicked himself. He should have gotten in the car and gone to her when she was in the hospital.

"Remember, she dumped you." Reason tried to pound some sense into his head. His communications over the past week with Twanna were clear; Kitty was done with him. The angry calls he'd had from the congressman were clearer; his job was in jeopardy.

"You got us into this mess." Reason took a shot at Phat Head.

"Stop!" Davis intervened before the war with himself resumed.

Lou had come over every day to see about him. She claimed it was to unpack and make sure he got settled. But with each visit his mother grew firmer in her position. She wasn't going to be happy if he left home again.

Davis rolled over and caught himself before he fell to the floor. Thanks to his mother, everything had a place in the house except him. He'd spent the nights between Christmas and now wandering between his bed, her room, and the sofa.

He sat up and bumped his head on the metal tiara-shaped headboard. The coolness of the wall art sent a chill through his body. He sat for a while in the same position, trying to decide if his house was cold or his heart. He'd worked so hard in the days since Kitty left to harden it.

She was wrong. She was immature. She wasn't ready for a normal adult relationship. It was fine with him that she went running back to daddy. She could stay with him for all he cared.

It wasn't right that he'd found out about her parents getting a divorce on the Internet. And their divorce shouldn't have impacted her like that; it wasn't her fault. Divorce was a serious bridge to cross, but with all that Roosevelt Franklin had done...

There had to be more to the story, and whatever it was, Kitty should have shared it with him. They could have faced it together. She didn't have to bear the burden alone. He lay back down and rubbed his head. His forehead felt hot.

"I'm not sick or lovesick, just tired from working twelve-hour days."

While school was out for winter break, there were a lot of children's programs to oversee at the Center. His unspoken hope was if he showed sufficient dedication to his job, Roosevelt wouldn't fire him. He knew he was probably wasting his energy. The man had threatened him a dozen times in the past week alone.

A glimpse of Glynnis at his fraternity's New Year's celebration danced across his memory. She might be a poorly dressed cougar, but she knew her event management. And in her congratulating herself for a job well done she'd let something slip. Glynnis had wanted his job for years and since she was drunk, she had let it slip that she was close to getting it.

He lay in his lonely place and listened to Luther as the clock inched forward. He really should have gone to Bible study tonight. As the church's newest deacon, he had obligations. His faith and work at the church would be his salvation. It was his faith that gave him the assurance that he'd survive the loss of his girl and his job.

"I wish Roosevelt would stop torturing me and just get on with it," he yelled. Silently, he prayed for Kitty to return just one of his calls. "Wasn't there supposed to be one final break-up call?" *If I could just talk to her.*

"Sing, Luther," he wailed to "Till My Baby Comes Home." Tonight the lyrics cleared the clouds from his head. All he needed was another chance to talk to her. "I'm the motivational speaker," he yelled. The heaviness of his voice pounded in his ears.

Luther sang while Davis mulled over a plan. If he got fired he could stay in Rock Hill. He'd use his contacts from church and the Gates

Foundation to run his motivational speaking business full time from Rock Hill. Luther's wailing continued with "Superstar."

"Dave, Dave," his mother's voice rang out over the stereo.

Before he could sit upright Lou found him and switched on the light, revealing his sorry state.

"Boy, what am I going to do with you?" Lou stepped closer to the bed. "Davis, wash up and come to the kitchen. Terri Taylor's here with me. She brought you something to eat. And stop with all this sorry singing. I'm sick of hearing it," she fussed.

Davis took a few minutes to move. He wasn't up for company. He and Luther had plans to make. Suddenly, Luther stopped singing. His mother had turned off his music, just as she had when he was younger and she'd fussed about Prince's inappropriate lyrics. The quiet forced him to acknowledge the rumble of his stomach. He trudged to the bathroom to run a hot wash cloth over his face while his plan solidified.

He stepped into his kitchen just as Terri pulled a beautiful golden brown chicken pot pie from a stay hot bag.

"Hi, Davis." She aimed a cheerful smile his way. "It was my turn to provide dinner for the Bible study group and I saved this pie just for you. I baked it fresh in the church's kitchen. Pastor barely let me get out the door with it." She shifted from foot to foot and gave a nervous chuckle.

"Terri, you shouldn't do things like this for me." He lumbered toward the makeshift table.

Terri's feet settled. "I remembered last week when you came to Bible study late and there wasn't anything left for you to eat. I wanted to make sure you had something to eat this week. Since you didn't make it to Bible study, I thought I should bring this pie over to you."

"Sit down and eat, son." Lou gestured from her seat at the card table.

Davis sat down and Terri served him. That's the kind of woman we need, Reason pushed him. Davis glanced over and noticed the sway of Terri's curvaceous hips as she stood by the stove. Just the right size for us, Phat Head put in. Davis picked up his fork and pricked the crust. The hot pie bubbled. The aroma of a lovingly cooked meal added to the emptiness in his heart. He looked up. "Thank you, thank you both."

Terri turned from the sink and beamed.

"I'll do those dishes, Terri, don't bother," he mumbled.

Lou shook her head in protest. "Let her help. Terri, if you don't mind?"

Terri nodded and went to her task.

Davis took a bite of the pie, then a few more. Lou must have given Terri some advice because the pie was perfect, with lots of meat. Before he scooped up the last bite, he paused.

"Mama, I hate to ask you to do anything else for me, but I need a decent kitchen table. Can you find one and get it? Even if it needs a little work, go ahead, get it and put it in Daddy's workshop. I'll fix it when I get back."

"Wait a minute." Lou's face contorted. "Where you going, son?"

"DC in the morning."

Lou pushed back, jarring the card table, and clapped her hands in joy. "She called!"

"No."

Lou's hands and face dropped. "He call you in for a meeting?"

The clank of dishes rose from the sink. Davis turned toward the sink where Terri held a cereal bowl aloft.

"No, ma'am. I'm going to get Kitty."

The bowl plopped into the sink.

"But what about what her father said?" Lou asked.

He stood and shoved his hands into his pockets. "I don't care. She's going to have to tell me off in person."

"You know Roosevelt Franklin doesn't make idle threats. Are you sure? Are you prepared to lose your job?" Deep concern furrowed Lou's brow.

Davis walked over and hugged her. "I don't care what it costs me."

The sound of water coursing down the drain filled the room. "Lou, I'm ready. Davis needs to pack for his trip."

He stepped over to the sink. "I'm not taking a bag. I plan to just go. I might be home tomorrow night."

Terri stepped back and gave him a rueful smile. "By faith, pack a bag."

His face erupted in the first genuine smile of the year. "Thank you, Terri, you've been a good friend to the family."

"And I'll continue to be when you get back with Kitty." She returned his smile.

Davis looked at the two good old-fashioned Southern women who cared for him. "You two are God's most gracious and compassionate creatures." He took a few steps toward Terri and embraced her. "Terri

Taylor, don't you give in until you find a man that's willing to come get you."

Terri stepped away from his hug and reached to gather her plate and bag. "I don't plan to."

He walked the ladies out to Terri's car. Before she stepped into the vehicle, Lou, grinning from ear to ear, reached up and gave him a hug. "I've been waiting for you to find the courage to mount up and go get Princess. She doesn't deserve anything less." Lou sat down in the car and rolled down the window. "You call as soon as you know."

Chapter 22

Davis sped through most of South Carolina and all of Virginia. He slowed as he approached the Maryland state line and thanked God he hadn't been pulled over. "Lord, make my way straight and give me the right words." This was the mantra that he recited before a speech. Today the words had become a chant, off and on during the morning.

Following the directions of his GPS, he crossed Military Road Northwest. It wouldn't be long before confrontation or reconciliation. At the intersection of Western and Broad Branch Roads a long red light caught him. He thought back to Thanksgiving Day when he and Kitty made this trip together. The tongue lashing she'd given him that day should have turned him off. No, it was the way she used her tongue that turned us on, Phat Head reminded him.

"Lord, make my way straight and give me the right words."

The light changed. He drove forward and made the right onto Aberfoyle Place, then parked in front of the Franklins' DC home. He sat for a while, praying. Then he just sat.

Why hesitate now? Reason asked. You drove like a madman to get here. Now go in and get her.

Yeah, man, let's go get our girl, Phat Head raged.

"At least I'm in agreement with myself," he muttered as he stepped away from his car.

Again, he stood at the door of the Franklin house filled with anticipation. He rubbed his hands together as Yesenia opened the door.

"Hello Davis? Why are you here?" she asked in a disinterested, weary way as she stepped back to let him in. "Did Twanna tell you she was here?"

"Yes, ma'am."

She rolled her eyes and glided into the living room.

"With all due respect, Mrs. Franklin, I'm not here to play any games. I've come to see Kitty." He followed her in.

"How much has Twanna told you?" she asked.

"Not much, but enough." He sank onto the sofa and glanced around the room that reminded him he was in the District and in a house filled with lies and hidden agendas.

"Can I get you anything?" She appeared tired.

"No, ma'am, I don't want to put you out. I just need to see Kitty."

Yesenia straightened her back and gave him a hard glare. He had to smile. Kitty made the same face when she was solid on a point. "I just got Kitty to settle down and take a nap."

"You speak like she's a child." His head turned toward the staircase. His upbringing kept him from charging up those stairs.

Yesenia stood and moved next to him on the sofa. "She's my baby. And she's more fragile than we thought. I know she talks a big game, but she's always had a sensitive soul."

His mustache twitched. He'd seen through her bravado on that first date.

"Davis, she's been through too much in the past few weeks. We've put her through too much and…" a tear formed in her eyes, "…I don't want to see her hurt anymore. I don't think she can bear it."

Davis stood. He wasn't the one out to hurt her.

"I'm sure you know about the posting of the divorce papers." Yesenia wrung her hands together.

He'd read through the blogs on Roosevelt Franklin on Christmas Day and Twanna filled in the personal details. Kitty had been clear about her obligation to protect her family, and her signature on her mother's divorce petition might mean an end to her father's career. "Yes, ma'am."

"She was only trying to be a good daughter to me. I should have never asked Kitty to draft my petition. I know plenty of attorneys, but she's the only one I thought I could trust. I asked too much of her. I've lived in Washington long enough to have known better. I should have shredded those papers."

Davis turned and studied her face. The bags under her eyes reminded him of a mother with a newborn.

"Davis, please tell me something. Why'd you break it off with her?"

He inhaled deeply. Based on all Kitty had told him about her mother, the question was unexpected. "Mrs. Franklin, Kitty's told me all about your family rule of not discussing details of relationships, and I agree with it. What's happened between Kitty and me is just between us. Now will you please let me see her?" He looked towards the stairs.

The front door flew open with a bang. "What are you doing here?" Roosevelt bellowed.

Davis stood and took a few steps back. The confrontation he dreaded was at hand. Lord, make my way straight and give me the right words.

"Well, it's just as well. I can do this face to face, save me a trip home. You're fired, and leave my daughter alone. You've hurt her enough. Boy, you better thank the Lord she wasn't hurt in that car. How dare you build up her hopes, then throw my Kitten out on the streets? I should've dismissed you sooner, and I would have if we didn't have Kitty to take care of. But since you're here now, you're fired. Get out!" Roosevelt threw his coat to the floor and stopped to catch his breath. "Well, go on, boy, get out and don't bother us, any of us, anymore."

"Rosey!" and "Daddy!" rang out in the same moment.

"Stop it, Daddy," Kitty yelled from the top of the stairs. Was it possible for those short legs to take the stairs two at a time? Within seconds she stood between him and her father. His mustache twitched and Davis held his breath. The lady had her tongue loaded to fire, and he hoped he wasn't the target.

"Mr. Franklin, I didn't come here to start a ruckus. I'd like your permission to just speak to Kitty."

"You're too nice, Davis. You don't need to ask him for anything." Kitty turned her flaring eyes toward him.

He took a step back. Maybe he was in the line of fire. He held his breath while she caught hers. Then it began. For several minutes the house was filled with general hollering. Kitty yelled at her father, her father yelled at her mother, and Yesenia yelled at them both. Davis stood back on his heels. For the first time the Franklins seemed normal; they were going at it in the same way his family did.

"That's it! I've had enough of this," Davis roared above the fray. "Kitty, I'll speak to you now. Alone."

Everything stopped.

Yesenia stepped around him and took her husband's arm. "We'll go into the kitchen. Come on, Rosey."

"Mommy, I feel dizzy." Kitty stumbled forward. "Davis, will you go with me upstairs? I need to lie down." She leaned into him and pleaded with her eyes for his strength.

Go ahead sweep her up and carry her up to the bedroom, Reason and Phat Head declared simultaneously.

※

Hours later Kitty yawned. "Davis, how long have I been asleep?"

He yawned, too. "I don't know. I must have dozed off. But not before I read your letter." He clutched a handful of papers that she'd been working on. A dozen handwritten pages, all addressed to him. "If your head still hurts we don't need to talk." He kissed her forehead and glanced around her teenage room.

She still had a Michael Jackson Off the Wall poster hanging.

He strengthened his hold on her. "I need you to understand that life's not going to be a fairy tale. We both have to make some major shifts for us to work."

"I know. When I grow up, can I please be Mrs. Davis Thornton?"

"Yeah." His grin widened. "But baby, we might have to wait a bit until I can build up enough steady business to support you. I don't have a job anymore."

Kitty sat up in bed and stretched. She giggled at his feet, which hung over the edge of her twin bed. "Me, either. Daddy fired me. And I think my mother made him do it."

"Y'all have the strangest family dynamics I've ever seen," he groaned. "But I'm glad that your mother has a policy of staying out of married folks' business." He rolled over and almost fell off the bed. "It's no way to start our lives together. With both of us unemployed."

She scrambled over him to the door and opened it. "Daddy, Daddy!" she yelled.

He leaped up and pushed the door closed. "Kitty, no! Not just two minutes ago you said you could be my grown-up wife. I don't want daddy's little girl. I don't expect you to shift overnight, but can't you go five minutes?" His mustache turned down a bit.

She turned and gave him her look, the one that neither he nor Roosevelt could defend against. "Just one more, Davis. He owes me big time. Daddy!"

Before he could protest an insistent rap beat on the door. "Kitty, honey, what's wrong?" Yesenia's concern penetrated the door.

Davis opened the door and she stepped in.

"What do you want with your father? I sent him out to get some champagne."

"Daddy fired Davis." Kitty stomped her foot.

"That? Is there anything else?" Her mother cocked her head to the side.

Kitty grinned, screamed, and hugged her mother. "He asked me to marry him."

Davis stepped back and let the little ladies hop and dance around the room. "Oh, joy!" Yesenia screamed. "When? Soon, I hope!"

Kitty stopped and plopped down on the bed.

Davis immediately went and sat by her side. She looked smaller and more delicate than usual.

"Mommy, we don't have jobs." She pushed her lips out.

"Children." Yesenia sat down on the bed with them. She reached out for both their hands. "There have been a lot of changes since Christmas that neither of you know about. I'm now the CEO of the Franklin Center." She turned to her daughter. "Do you think I'd fire Davis?" Then she turned toward him. "Son, that job is yours for as long as you want it. And I hope that's for a long, long time." She released their hands and stood. "Now you two come downstairs. Your father is prepared now to speak with Davis. And we have so much to do." She stopped at the door with a broad smile covering her face. "Kitty, I've got hundreds of calls to make. Mama Cat, your sisters, your mother," she nodded toward Davis, "and the rest of the family. Kitty, call Twanna, although I think she already knows," Yesenia babbled while they lay back on the bed and laughed.

Chapter 23

Kitty, Yesenia, and Louvinia found seats in the Franklin living room, exhausted after their second consecutive day searching bridal shops.

"Kitty, why can't you just wait? So we can plan things properly," Yesenia complained.

"I agree," Lou said, reaching down to rub her tired feet. "You need to give us all more time."

"No, I want to hurry up and marry Davis before I say something that will make him change his mind." Kitty sat next to the woman who would become her mother-in-law in less than a week. "Everything is going to work out, I just know it."

They had fewer than five days to get everything in order, including finding the perfect dress. Kitty was dead set on marrying Davis on Martin Luther King Day and was pushing hard to make it happen.

Roosevelt's shadow darkened the entry of the living room. For days her father had been barking orders at his congressional staff to ensure the special use permits for Kitty and Davis to marry at the Washington Monument were obtained. He did it all from under a dark cloud, and since she was no longer his confidant, Kitty didn't know why.

"What does she want now?" he bellowed.

"Nothing, Rosey." Yesenia looked over at her husband. They'd called an armistice for the wedding.

"Give her anything she wants," he barked. "And, Mrs. Thornton, about the reception you want to throw the children in Rock Hill. You'll have to ask your son how he wants to handle that since I'm no longer in charge. Just make sure Mrs. Franklin agrees." He stomped out of the living room.

Lou's mouth flew open.

Yesenia stood up and called after her husband, "Rosey, wait." She sighed. "Excuse me," she said and followed him out of the room.

Kitty sat in the window seat in her room later, thinking about her father. As promised, her father had taken good care of her. He'd found a migraine headache expert at Johns Hopkins to review her medical case. The new doctor prescribed a new medication and a dose of meditation. She stretched. In time the new medicine should put an end to her debilitating headaches, but she still had some problems. Every afternoon she had to stop and have at least an hour of down time. During her hour she'd think and pray. Today she thought about her father; old habits died hard.

Kitty inhaled. "Daddy is in good hands."

Kitty exhaled. The new media consultant she'd hired was excellent. He'd taken the divorce petition story and spun it so expertly that her father's re-election campaign got a bump in the polls.

First, he let the story run its course. The twenty-four-hour news cycle was just that, twenty-four hours. On Christmas Eve he contacted all of his sources and pointed out the obvious. There were no court stamps on the documents everyone had downloaded and flashed before the cameras the day before. Yesenia Franklin had not filed for divorce. Along with the obvious, he used Yurgay's report to plant suspicion that the documents were created by the political action committee made up of key South Carolina republicans that owned the website removeRooseveltFranklin.com. Then he released a photograph of Roosevelt Franklin escorting his fragile wife into the hospital on Christmas Day to visit their blinded daughter.

Kitty stared out her window at the Washington Monument. It was time for her to leave the District. She was just an amateur in the high stakes game of politics and media image. In a million years she couldn't have made the moves her father's new team, lead by the media consultant, had. While she was in the hospital they dispatched Uncle Tom to Capitol Hill to warn key legislators of the celebrity trash picking. That move brought Roosevelt a few favors. Then the media consultant placed the ex-lobbyist turned trash picker on retainer. And on New Years Eve he closed by issuing a press release that Catherine Franklin's sight was restored and she was resting comfortably at home with her parents.

Kitty shook her head and picked up her prayer and meditation journal. "I'm looking forward to a simpler life."

On a clear, cold Washington morning Kitty married Davis at the base of the Washington Monument. It had cost her father some political capital since it was a national holiday, and the wedding was pulled together on such short, short notice. Kitty turned and smiled at everyone who'd gathered to celebrate their marriage. Underneath Lou's broad smile, a hint of sorrow. She'd received a call just before she left the hotel this morning that Charlie had passed during the night. Although he knew he'd never make it, Uncle Charlie wouldn't rest until Ralph purchased his ticket to DC for his favorite nephew's wedding. His greatest concern in the last week of his life was not to die on Davis's wedding day. He'd passed shortly before midnight.

"Look over there, Aunt Kitty." Quanny pointed in the direction of the photographer and smiled for the photo. Quanny wore the same white flower girl dress she would wear for her father's wedding in less than a month. As Yvette said, the only change required to the dress would be to replace the sweetheart pink sash with a royal purple one for today's ceremony.

Her parents stood as they always did, together but not close. Next to Rev. and Mrs. Gates, Davis's friends from Chicago. The only request Davis made was that his friend Finus Gates perform the ceremony and that his wife Cassandra sing.

Her bridesmaids Yvette, Dena, and Twanna shivered and chatted with Dena's boyfriend Levi while Uncle Tom and his wife headed toward their car.

Davis grinned and shivered through all of the photos. She felt a little sorry for her husband and offered to let him share the warmth of the white mink coat he'd given her as a wedding gift.

As soon as the photographer snapped the final picture, Davis pulled at Kitty's hand.

"We'll see you all in a few. Wave bye-bye, Mrs. Thornton."

After they waved goodbye to their small wedding party Davis led her to the entrance of the Monument. They stepped inside and followed the directions of security. Even though she'd been inside the Monument just twenty minutes ago with her family while they waited for the wedding to start, the guards insisted that now they follow protocol.

"What are you doing, Dave? We're going to delay the breakfast."

"They'll wait on us. After all, we're the guests of honor." He beamed.

"Congratulations." The park ranger tipped his hat as they stepped toward the golden elevator.

She stared at Davis. "This isn't a part of what Daddy negotiated. We can't go up today."

"Yes, we can. Now come on, you just promised to follow me along the way." He winked at the words Rev. Gates had used to replace the old-fashioned love, honor, and obey. "We haven't been married ten good minutes and you're already giving me lip."

Kitty snapped her lips together and looked around. It was a bit of a special treat to actually be inside the Washington Monument. Despite his sour mood over the past week, her father had really come through. By special orders she'd been allowed to have a short ceremony at the base of the monument.

"I don't suppose you two want the standard tour facts," the park ranger said as they stepped inside the gilded elevator that would take them to the observation deck.

"I would," Davis said. He squeezed her hand as they began the ninety-second ascent.

The historical facts went over Kitty's head. The doors opened five hundred feet above the ground.

"Watch your step," the ranger said as they stepped out of the elevator and onto the observation deck. "You've got about ten private minutes before the nine o'clock tour group joins you. But since it's the King holiday, I'm not sure the tour will be full."

Kitty stepped forward along the narrow corridor. She looked around at the unfamiliar halls.

"Mrs. Thornton, when was the last time you actually came up here?"

"Mr. Thornton, I'm so full and happy today, I really can't remember if I've ever been up here."

"I didn't think so, because as much as you talk about the Monument you never said anything about the inside. Come over here. I've got something for you."

He led her to the north side of the observation deck and they peered out of the small windows.

"Wow, that's a great view of the White House," Kitty exclaimed. "And Davis, see that field? That's where they display the national Christmas tree. We'll have to come back during Christmas for you to see it again."

"Okay, now step over here please, ma'am." They walked toward the west viewing windows.

Looking west Kitty pointed out the Reflecting Pool and the bridge to Arlington before he directed her to the south.

Kitty exclaimed at the view across the Potomac and pointed out the Lincoln Memorial. "Davis, let's come back this spring. You'll love it. DC is so beautiful when the cherry blossoms are in full bloom."

"If they are half as lovely as you are today. I can't wait." He bent over and kissed the top of her head. "Come on." He nudged her forward on their tour.

"I'm so glad you brought me up here today." She beamed.

"There's more."

They moved over to the east view.

As she looked east Davis spoke in that melodic, rich, and strong voice that soothed and reassured her. "From here you can see the Capitol. I think it's fitting that I say this to you now."

She looked up at his serious face and waited through his speaker's pause.

"Kitty, when we were apart I thought a lot about dichotomy, pairs, and being able to be two things at one time. I struggled with trying to understand how you could love your father and your mother when it seemed their values were so disparate. And I didn't know how you could be true to me and your father at the same time. And you know what I discovered?" He took a deep breath. "Maybe we aren't giving dichotomy its due. It's just like the views we're enjoying. One small observation deck, but two distinctly different views from the north and west."

Kitty nodded.

"There is our relationship and the relationship between you and your father, yet there's just one of you. I accept now that you can love him and me. And two can be one. Our lives have just become one, and I'm looking forward to every day with you."

"Me, too."

"Shh. What I brought you up here to say, Kitty Thornton, is that you gave me a new perspective on life and love and I want to give you one as a wedding gift."

She cocked her head to the side and smiled at him. She wouldn't dare open her mouth again until he finished.

"Kitty, for a long time you've looked to the outward symbol of this Monument for perspective. But I'd like you to look out today to a new perspective. They say if you strain your neck just right you can see the ocean. Know that you have unlimited potential and opportunities as vast as the view to the east. And know that you have a whole ocean of love coming from me and our family."

She nodded and took a deep breath. His words, as usual, were going straight to her soul.

"Kitty, all the time you spent looking at the outside I bet you didn't know what it says on the top, above us, what you couldn't see. Maybe what you've been drawing strength from all these years is an inscription. They say it was ordered to be placed there by George Washington himself."

Her eyes widened.

"Laus Deo," he said. "It means…"

"Praise be to God," she finished. She'd intended to keep quiet, but old habits die hard. "Right over our heads? I never knew. For real, Davis?"

"Yes, it's inscribed on the cap."

"Wow, I didn't know that, but now it all makes sense, my love." She took his large hand in hers. She turned his hand so that she could see the platinum and diamond ring she'd placed there an hour ago. "Now I have a surprise for you. I prayed while we were apart. I didn't have anyone else I could talk to. There wasn't anyone I wanted to talk to, so I learned to talk to God. My faith isn't strong, but I promised God to praise him if you came back to me. I even started praising him before you came to get me. Laus Deo!" she shouted. "Laus Deo!"

Davis laughed. "You've shifted. Go ahead, Kitty Thornton, praise God and always know that I believe in you."

Authors Note

Rock Hill, South Carolina was the actual setting of an important event in civil rights history. In February 1961, ten African-American men went to jail for staging a sit-in at the segregated McCrory's lunch counter. Instead of following the usual practice of arrest, lock-up, and bail-out, nine members of this group pioneered a new strategy called "jail, no bail." Jail, no bail shifted the cost of demonstrating. Instead of the financially stapped civil rights organizations providing bail money, the cost shifted. The authorities were now forced to pay for jail space and food.

The men are known as the Friendship Nine because eight of the nine men were students at Rock Hill's Friendship Junior College. They are also referred to as the Rock Hill Nine.

In creating Roosevelt Franklin I explored an unspoken reality of the civil rights story. Everyone didn't participate in the movement. And many who attended organizing meetings never show up for the protest.

About the Author

In 2004, **Regena Bryant** made a pact with her nephew. "If you give me a college degree, I'll write a book." For the next five years she actively worked on crafting. *Believe in Me*, is her second novel.

Regena lives in suburban Chicago with her husband, children, and her nephew's college diploma.

Visit her website at www.regenabryant.com.